POWER OF THE WITCH

WITCHES OF KEATING HOLLOW, BOOK 7

DEANNA CHASE

ABOUT THIS BOOK

Welcome to Keating Hollow, the enchanted village full of love, family, and magic.

Shannon Ansell didn't mean to make a bet with Brian Knox. It sort of just happened. Now she's agreed to date him for six weeks, the one man she knows she shouldn't. Six dates in six weeks. She can do that and still keep her heart intact, right? Wrong. Because the only thing she can't resist more than a good bet is Brian Knox.

CHAPTER 1

Shannon Ansell sat in the shadows, sipping her champagne and wishing she was anywhere other than Jacob Burton and Yvette Townsend's wedding reception. It wasn't that she hated weddings... Well, maybe she did. But that had more to do with her personal feelings about getting married than it did the actual party. And she had to admit Jacob and Yvette's party was an excellent one.

Floating fairy lights lit up the patio space of A Touch of Magic, the upscale spa that Faith Townsend owned. Magical instruments played seemingly on their own off in the corner while the guests danced in the cool summer night. The reception was an elegant, intimate affair that suited Yvette and Jacob perfectly. Shannon would be up and out on the dance floor swaying to the music right at that moment if she hadn't vowed to never show her face again. Not after the night before. It was too embarrassing. She'd seriously thought about not showing up at all for the reception, but since she'd catered the desserts and made the cake, bailing hadn't been an option.

"Hey, girlfriend." Hope Scott slid into the chair next to

Shannon, placing a piece of cake in front of her. "Eat up before it's all gone."

Shannon wrinkled her nose and shook her head. She knew it was good. Better than good. Excellent even. Yvette wouldn't have hired her to make it if it wasn't. But Shannon was in no mood to eat anything. "I'm sticking with champagne, thanks."

"Trying to drink enough to forget about the bachelorette party last night?" Hope asked with a light chuckle. "I think you can relax. It wasn't that bad."

Shannon stared into the heart-shaped face of the pretty blonde and let out a choked huff of incredulous laughter. "Not that bad? Just stop. I was giving instructions for a perfect blow job with an actual dildo when Brian and Jacob walked in. Worse, I didn't even know Brian was there until I got to the deep throat portion of the lesson. I think I need to move. Maybe I can find a job at a bakery somewhere in Europe. You think that's far enough?"

"Nope. Not after what I heard. I'll just follow you." Brian's amused voice cut through the darkness.

"That's my cue to find Chad," Hope said, referring to her fiancé. She shot up out of her chair, grinning at Shannon, and mouthed, *Take him home with you.*

Shannon ignored her. No way. Never gonna happen. She turned toward Brian and groaned when she saw his handsome face emerge from the shadows. "Go away. Your chance to experience that particular talent expired a few months ago."

"My loss." He sat down in the empty seat Hope had vacated and draped an arm over the back of Shannon's chair.

Yeah it was. Her face burned as she remembered the night she'd thrown herself at him and he'd rejected her. What the hell had she been thinking? She hadn't. That was the problem. She couldn't even blame it on the wine. Two glasses

2

hadn't been enough to render her reckless. No, she'd been having a good time on their date and hadn't wanted it to end. She'd thought he felt the same, but the moment clothes had started to come off, he'd bolted. She hadn't heard from him again until earlier in the week when she'd stupidly agreed to *the bet*.

Six dates in six weeks. He had to figure out what she enjoyed on a date and make it happen. If just one date went sideways, he had to be her pool boy... *in a thong...* until the end of October. If all the dates were successful and Brian won the bet, she had to pretend to be his fiancée at a family wedding. Plus, she'd have to give him a massage... *with both of them naked.*

Gah! What was she, a masochist? Yes. The answer was definitely yes. What other explanation did she have for agreeing to such a ridiculous bet?

"So. Tomorrow night. Be ready at six. I'll pick you up at your house," he said.

She side-eyed him. "What makes you think I'm free on such short notice?"

His dark eyes twinkled in the moonlight. "I have my ways."

"You're a cocky bastard." Shannon stifled a chuckle. She wanted to be mad, but she just couldn't. Usually she taught a yoga class on Sunday night, but it just so happened her class had been moved to the morning that week. The fact that he knew that meant he had been doing his homework.

"That's one of the many reasons you like me." He winked and, without asking, stole a bite of her untouched cake.

"That's one of the many reasons you annoy me." But the smile on her face betrayed her.

He laughed. "Right. I can see that."

She rolled her eyes, but the truth was she was far from annoyed. And her earlier inclination to stay hidden in the shadows had fled. Brian Knox was making her feel all tingly inside, just as he had during their first date.

Dammit.

She wasn't supposed to be enjoying him. He was trouble with a capital T. The type of man who loved to date her but ran for the hills when any talk of commitment or relationship came into play. She'd been through it before, and she was tired of that game. Done with it in fact.

From there on out, she was only supposed to be dating men who wanted something more. She was ready for a partner. Brian Knox wasn't. He'd told her as much on the one and only date they'd shared a few months ago.

If she recalled correctly, his exact words were, *To be honest, Shannon, I'm not the relationship type. That road always leads to trouble.*

It was then she decided that he'd be her last fling. Her one last temptation. He was just too sexy.

Then when things were just heating up, he'd bolted, mumbling something about needing to get up early in the morning. She'd felt confused, rejected, and empty inside. She'd vowed to swear off guys like Brian that night and only date men actively looking for a relationship. Unfortunately, her dating life since then had bored her out of her mind. It had been after a particularly awful date with a healer from Eureka, who spent the entire night defending a dissertation on potions to clear warts, that she'd broken down and made that stupid bet with Brian.

She'd been in a weakened state. What could she say? A girl deserved a little fun, didn't she? If nothing else, their fake dates would be amusing. It didn't mean she had to give up on trying to find her forever someone, did it?

She'd think about that tomorrow. Tonight, she suddenly wanted to dance.

"Hey, Brian," she started.

He'd just turned to her when a husky male voice cut through the darkness. "Hey, Brian. Get a move on. This one is waiting for you."

Shannon turned her attention to the temporary bar and spotted a gorgeous man with light brown hair, golden skin, and a sexy smile that was to die for. Beside him, there was a petite, blue-eyed blonde smiling in Brian's direction. The woman reminded Shannon of a pixie, a sharp contrast to Shannon's shocking red hair, brown eyes, and her almost six-foot frame.

"Right," Brian said with a nod. He turned his attention back to Shannon. "What was it you were going to say?"

"Nothing. Nothing at all." She'd be damned if she was going to admit she was about to ask him to dance.

He narrowed his eyes, studying her.

Shannon raised one eyebrow in challenge.

But he didn't take the bait. He just chuckled and said, "All right, gorgeous. See you tomorrow night at six."

"How should I dress for this date?" she asked, knowing he wasn't going to give her many details.

He let his gaze roam over her body, his lips curving into a predatory grin. "Something sexy."

"Of course," she said dryly, imagining he was going to take her to dinner and dancing. To be fair, that plan would fit the qualifications for a date she'd enjoy. Shannon loved to dance. But she'd hoped he'd put a little imagination into wherever he decided to take her.

"Goodnight, Shannon." He leaned over and barely brushed

his lips over her cheek. Then he crossed the patio and immediately snaked his arm around the waist of the pixie.

Guh! Shannon turned away so she didn't have to see him flirting with someone else. She knew it shouldn't bother her. They were not a couple. And there was no chance they'd be a couple at the end of this bet. They were just going to be friends. Maybe. But nothing more.

"Is this seat taken?"

Shannon turned her attention to the man who'd called Brian over to the bar. The moonlight shone down on him, highlighting his long dark eyelashes and making Shannon catch her breath. Heaven help her. He was gorgeous, and she couldn't stop herself from staring. While Brian was tall, dark, and sexy with a rugged scar in one eyebrow, this creature had light eyes that danced with humor and an inviting smile that came with the kind of face one could stare at for hours and never get bored. Son of a... where had Jacob found all his friends? Hotties R Us?

"Shannon?" he asked.

"Huh?" She blinked, trying to clear her stupid brain fog.

"Is this seat taken?"

"Um, no." She waved a hand, indicating he should take a seat.

"Thanks." He held a hand out. "We haven't met yet. I'm Rex Holiday, friend of the groom."

"Shannon Ansell. Friend of the bride... sort of."

"Sort of?" He laughed, the deep rumble oddly inviting. She'd have to make him do that again. "What does that mean?" he asked. "Frenemies?"

"Sort of." She let out a chuckle of her own. "We've known each other for years. I wouldn't call us friends necessarily, but Yvette did trust me to cater the desserts. Her sister Abby and I

6

kinda had a rivalry in school that ended up extending to all of the Townsend sisters. They tend to stick together. But maybe we're old enough now that it doesn't matter so much."

"You made those sea salt caramels that are in the shape of books?" he asked, sounding impressed.

"Yep. Yvette and Jacob own a bookstore together. It seemed fitting."

"Well, Shannon Ansell, I can't think of anything I'd rather do than dance with the local chocolatier. What do you say? Will you let me lead you around the dance floor?" He stood and held out his hand.

Shannon glanced at Brian, who had his head bent down to the pixie's as she whispered something in his ear. Hot irritation shot up her spine, but she ignored it as she placed her hand in Rex's and said, "I thought you'd never ask."

CHAPTER 2

*T*he faint scent of strawberries surrounded Brian as Cara leaned in, pressing her palm to his biceps. She was chuckling over a story she'd been telling that involved the beach, her best friend, and a wardrobe malfunction. Normally he'd be giving his undivided attention to anyone talking about a half-naked woman, but his gaze was riveted to the dance floor where Rex freakin' Holiday had just wrapped his arms around Shannon.

My Shannon. The thought flashed through his mind, forcing him to suppress a frustrated groan.

Brian hadn't been able to get her out of his mind ever since that night she'd beckoned him to her bed and he'd run away like a pimply preteen who was too inexperienced to understand what was being offered.

That was the problem. He knew all too well what would've happened if he'd allowed himself to slide between the sheets with the curvy redhead. They would've had a smoking hot month together, and then he would've ended it. Just like he'd ended all of his recent relationships because commitment was a four-letter word.

And now she'd written him off. He couldn't blame her. He'd gone from hot to cold so fast she'd probably suffered freezer burn.

The music switched to a slow song, and Brian's eyes narrowed as he watched Rex pull Shannon in tight against him. He pressed his cheek against hers, said something to make her face light up in a smile, and then ran a light hand down her bare arm.

Bastard. Brian's entire body tensed, and he wondered if anyone would notice if Rex Holiday suddenly disappeared. Probably. The man was supposed to be doing some seasonal work in town, helping the Pelshes with their new vineyard. The guy was a talented earth witch who specialized in creating strong small-scale farms.

Besides, Rex had been a friend since his college days. Brian loved the guy, but that didn't mean that he didn't want to sucker punch him for pawing Shannon.

"Brian?" Cara asked, pressing her small hand to his cheek. "Where'd you go?"

He jerked his attention back to the woman who was practically sitting on his lap. Shifting off the stool, he placed his hands on her hips to keep her from stumbling. "Sorry, Cara, gotta stretch the legs."

She stared up at him, her bright blue eyes searching. "What's wrong?"

"Nothing," he lied while trying not to stare at Shannon and Rex. "Why?"

"You seem… distracted."

Hell yes, he was distracted, but he wasn't going to talk to her about it. "I'm fine. Just thinking about a work project."

Her expression cleared, and she gave him a bright smile. "Oh, the one for my father?"

"Sure," he said, because that was the only project on the books at the moment.

"I can't wait for the spa opening. I already ordered a dress from Bella Ballarini. Her designs are to die for. I was thinking something romantic and lacy. That would be fitting for an upscale, new age spa, right?"

"Yeah. It would," he said, not caring in the least.

"You'll show me the layout designs tonight when we get back to your place, right? My dad wanted my initial opinion."

He ground his teeth together. He could hardly say no. Just like he hadn't been able to say no to letting her stay in his guest room. She'd invited herself while he'd been on a call with her old man. Robert Manchester had let out a bark of laughter and said, "Of course you'll stay with him. You two are dating, aren't you? The man isn't stupid."

Cara giggled and said she'd get packing, while Brian had gone into shock. When exactly had the old man decided he and Cara had started dating? Brian hadn't even been in Los Angeles for over a year. He'd offered to let her be his date at Jacob's wedding, but that was only after she'd pouted about not knowing anyone except Brian and Jacob.

Once she'd left the call, Manchester turned serious. "She likes you, Knox. When are you going to propose?"

"Propose?" Brian sputtered. "What are you talking—?"

"No need to act surprised, man. Once you two are married, you'll come work directly for me and eventually take over the company. It just makes sense, especially since the Knox and Manchester corporations have gone into partnership."

Manchester was talking about the upscale hotel business Brian's father owned and Manchester's luxury spas. The two men had been friends for years, and it was no secret that the families were interested in Brian and Cara making a match. But this was the first time anyone had actually come out and acted like it was something more than just wishful thinking.

Brian opened his mouth to firmly deny that there would be any sort of engagement, but before he could get the words out, Manchester's voice boomed over the line. "Gotta go, kid. We'll discuss the details later."

The line went dead, and Brian stared at his phone in pure irritation. He'd known he shouldn't have taken a job that involved dealing with Manchester. Brian vaguely wondered if his old man had gotten together with the spa owner and secretly worked out some sort of deal if Brian married Cara. The idea was entirely possible. Brian's old man was a manipulative bastard when he needed to be. There was a reason he didn't work for him.

"Brian," Cara whined. "When are you going to ask me to dance?"

Brian took a full step back, needing to put space between them. The memory of being pushed toward marrying her was far too fresh. The last thing he wanted to do was put his arms around her. Not when he needed to cross the dance floor and send Rex packing. But he couldn't turn Cara down and then immediately ask someone else to dance without looking like a grade A jackass. Suppressing a sigh, he held out his hand. "Care to dance, Cara?"

She beamed. "I thought you'd never ask."

He didn't answer her, because the truth was, he wouldn't have asked if it weren't for Shannon and Rex. Brian grabbed one of her hands and tugged her out onto the dance floor.

"That's better," she said, smiling up at him. "Now we're getting somewhere."

Right, we definitely are, he thought as he twirled her around in the direction of Shannon and Rex.

"Whoa. Who knew you were such a Fred Astaire?" Falling right into step with him, her eyes gleamed with excitement. "Did you take dance lessons as a kid or something?"

"Or something," he said, gliding her backward, not really wanting to talk about his training. His mother had been on Broadway before she'd met his father and all but forced her kids to study the arts. He'd gone for music and dance in his formative years. At the time, he'd been resentful of the jazz, ballet, and contemporary classes because he'd wanted to spend all his time with the cool kids in the hip hop classes and play the electric guitar. Instead, while he was allowed to take those classes, he'd spent a lot more time playing the piano and performing in jazz numbers the school produced. Looking back, he was grateful for the experience. It taught him a lot, even if he'd never really been interested in the performance life. Blowing Shannon's mind with his moves would be enough… if he ever got her back in his arms.

"Well, when it's our turn, we'll knock their socks off." She did some sort of complicated foot work, combined with a hip shimmy that screamed she'd had years of training, too.

"There isn't going to be an 'our turn,' Cara," he said gruffly and then unceremoniously walked away from her to tap on Rex's shoulder.

"Hey, Brian. What's up?" his friend said with an easy smile.

"Mind if I cut in?" He winked at Shannon, who was standing beside Rex with her arms crossed over her chest.

"Um, sure." He glanced at Shannon. "You don't mind, do you?"

Brian raised an eyebrow, challenging her to say no. If she really didn't want to dance with him, he'd walk away, but he'd make it his mission to have her in his arms the next night. He could see the hesitation in her expression, but before she could reject him, he offered her his hand. "Let's show them how it's done."

Interest sparked in her whiskey-colored eyes and he knew he had her. Grinning, he stepped forward, placed one hand on her hip, and tugged on the other one, pulling her into his body.

"Are you sure you want to do this?" she whispered in his ear. "Your date over there looks a little put out."

Brian didn't even glance back at Cara before he said, "She's not the one I want to hold against me for the rest of the night."

Shannon snorted out a laugh. "And I am?"

He stared down at her, his gaze intense on hers. "Shannon, if I had my way, I'd take you back to my place and plaster myself against your curvy body and stay that way for forty-eight hours. But since I know you'll roll your eyes and tell me I missed my chance, I'll just have to settle for dancing."

She frowned at him and glanced over his shoulder. "If this is how you treat your dates, I'm not sure you deserve six weeks of my time."

Her words made him feel as if a bucket of ice water had been dumped over his head. Is that really what she thought of him? Of course she did. Why wouldn't she? Cara *had* been his date after all. They'd shown up together, sat together, and even danced just a moment ago. Why would Shannon think any differently? "She's just a family friend, Shan. Trust me. There's nothing there. Our parents are in business together."

"I see." Her frown disappeared, but the slight suspicion in her tone was still noticeable.

"You don't believe me." It was statement, not a question.

"Can you blame me? I don't have the best track record with men."

"I don't have the best track record with women either, so I completely understand," he said. "But I think if we both let our guards down a little, we just might find something worth the effort."

He was rewarded with a tiny smile as she asked, "Oh, like what?"

"Like this." He raised her hand and twirled her around just once before pulling her back into his embrace as he wrapped his arms around her. He bent his head, bringing his lips right to hers so they were less than an inch apart.

Shannon's breathing hitched as she stared at his lips.

The desire to claim her was right there at the surface. All he could think about was tasting her again, owning her with his kiss. But something told him this had to be her choice. She'd already made it clear she didn't really trust him, and he didn't want to send her running. Instead, he placed a tiny bit of pressure on her lower back and whispered, "Shannon, kiss me."

There was no hesitation. She pressed up on her tiptoes, and when her soft lips brushed over his, Brian clutched her tighter, waiting. And when her tongue touched his, he was gone. He buried one hand in her thick red hair and gave her everything he had.

CHAPTER 3

*S*hannon sat at a table in the back of Incantation Café. She'd just got done teaching her yoga class and was staring into her lukewarm mocha as she let out a breathy sigh. Good gracious. Could Brian dance or what? She didn't think she'd ever been twirled quite like that before. And she could still feel Brian's lips on hers more than twelve hours later. Holy hell. That kiss had been everything. Her fingers and toes had even started tingling.

"Uh-oh. Sounds like trouble," a familiar female voice said.

Shannon glanced up to see Hope—formerly known as Luna—Scott standing over her table. Her honey blond hair had been pulled back into a neat bun and she was wearing yoga pants and a polo shirt with the *A Touch of Magic* logo, indicating she was likely on a break from work.

"Mind if I join you?" Hope asked, her big green eyes full of sympathy.

"Sure. Why not." Shannon waved a hand at the chair across from her.

Hope didn't say anything for a moment while she sipped

17

her chai tea latte. She leaned one arm on the table and studied Shannon in that quiet way of hers, making Shannon squirm a little.

"Just say it," Shannon said, shaking her head. She knew the other woman had something on her mind, and waiting for her to finally spit it out was akin to torture. Shannon wasn't one to keep her opinions to herself, and she much appreciated when her friends just spoke their minds.

Hope placed her cup on the table and tilted her head to one side, studying Shannon. "You're sitting here wondering what to do about Brian, aren't you?"

Shannon choked out a laugh. "What gave it away? The fact that I bolted out of the wedding reception right after he laid that kiss on me or the dopey look on my face every time someone asks me about him?"

"You don't have a dopey look now," Hope said with a half shrug.

"No? Just irritation then?"

She chuckled. "That's closer. But when you sighed right before I sat down, you definitely had that I'm-in-so-much-trouble vibe going on. Want to talk about it?"

"What's there to say? He's hot as hell, emotionally unavailable, and likely to dump me the moment I let him catch me. He's every mistake I've ever made, and I still can't help myself from being excited about tonight's date. Not to mention, he brought that pixie of a blonde to Yvette's wedding, and she was not happy with him after we played tonsil hockey on the dance floor. I do not want to get in the middle of something. I don't do drama."

Hope tore off a piece of her croissant and said, "Sounds like you have plenty to say on the subject."

Shannon scowled at her. "You're not being helpful."

"I know. I'm sorry. It's just obvious to me that you like him. What's so wrong with taking a chance and seeing where it goes?"

Because I'll get my heart broken... again, Shannon thought. But instead of voicing her truth she said, "I don't want to get emotionally invested in someone who clearly isn't interested in the long-term. It's a waste of time."

Hope nodded. "Sure. I can see that. But you have that six-week bet going on, so you might as well enjoy it, right?" Her lips curved up into a sly smile. "There's nothing wrong with having a little fun with Mr. Hotter Than Hell."

Oh, there was plenty wrong with having fun with him. She'd be paying for it in six weeks when he went his way and she went hers. Still, Hope's words sent a zing of anticipation straight up her spine. Oh, son of the devil. There was no way she was going to make it through the rest of the summer without ripping his clothes off. "You know what, Hope Scott?"

"What?"

"I think I liked you better when you kept most of your opinions to yourself."

"Liar," Hope said, laughing. "You love me just the way I am."

"That's true," Shannon said with a shrug. The two of them had bonded pretty quickly since Shannon could relate to Hope feeling like an outsider in Keating Hollow. Hope hadn't grown up in the magical town, and even though she now knew she was related to the Townsend sisters, they were still working on building those relationships. And Shannon had been the bad girl in high school who was caught skipping classes and hanging out with the wrong crowd from the coast. She'd never figured out how to make friends with the other girls in town. Her relationship with her parents had always been strained. The one person she'd felt closest to, her grandmother, had died her junior year in high school, and after that it was easier to keep everyone at arm's length.

Hope finished off her croissant and said, "I'm just saying that Brian seems like a cool guy. If I were you, I'd consider giving him a chance."

"Do I have competition now?" a man with a gravelly voice asked as he walked up to the table.

Shannon glanced up at the tall man, taking in his blond hair and light eyes. He was gorgeous in a clean-cut, all-American type way. He had always reminded Shannon of the star-quarterback type, only he was actually a classically trained pianist who'd been kind of a big deal until he retired from the concert circuit the year before.

"Nope. Not even close." Hope jumped out of her chair and planted a kiss on his lips. "Don't think you can get rid of me that easily."

"I wouldn't dream of it." He winked at her and slipped an arm around her waist as they both turned to look down at Shannon.

She looked past the love birds and nodded at Levi, Hope's brother. He'd followed Chad into the café and stood a few feet back with his hands in his pockets. The sixteen-year-old kid wore dark denim jeans that were ripped in the knees and a vintage Stones T-shirt. Shannon couldn't help but approve of his fashion choices. It was a solid look for the lanky teenager.

Levi nodded back. "Hey, Shannon."

"Hey, yourself." Shannon waved a hand at the chair Hope had just vacated. "Have a seat."

He slipped into Hope's chair and glanced at Chad. "Can you get me a mocha?"

"Sure, kid." Chad tugged Hope with him over to the café's

counter where they bent their heads together, talking while Hanna Pelsh waited on the man in line ahead of them.

Shannon turned her attention to Levi. "How's Keating Hollow treating you?"

Levi was new in town, having only started living with Hope that summer when she'd given him a place to stay after he'd been kicked out of their biological father's house. Since then she'd gotten legal custody of him, so he was there to stay. "Not bad. I'm taking some online classes until school starts this fall, and in the meantime, I'm helping Chad at his music store, running the register a few days a week while he gives private lessons."

"Really? So you're more than just muscle?" she asked, chuckling. Levi had spent quite a bit of time helping Chad with the store opening. The heavy lifting had been good for him. He'd noticeably bulked up since he'd arrived in town.

Levi raised his thin arms and flexed. "What do you mean? These guns are magic."

Shannon cracked up. "You're the best, kid. How's the store doing anyway? Has Keating Hollow turned into a music mecca?"

He shrugged. "Not exactly, but Chad seems pleased with how it's going so far. I, on the other hand, need more hours. Since the store can't support that yet, I've opened up a business doing yard work. Know anyone who needs help weeding and mowing?"

Shannon sat up straighter. She'd lost her yard guy two months ago when he moved south. "Yes. Me. When can you start?"

Levi raised his eyebrows. "You sound desperate."

"I am desperate. The weeds are taking over, and my front yard is starting to resemble a jungle."

"This afternoon?"

"Perfect." She sat back in her chair and smiled. "If it's a good fit, I'll hire you for weekly maintenance. Sound good?"

"Sounds perfect." His smile matched hers. "You'll be my first customer."

"If you do a good job, I'll spread the word at the chocolate shop. So… do a good job, all right?" Shannon knew he would. He was just that kind of kid. Levi hadn't ever had anything handed to him. He wouldn't expect this to be either.

"I will. No doubt about it. And if I miss something you want done, don't hesitate to let me know."

"You're on." She reached her hand across the table, offering it to him.

Levi immediately took her hand in his and shook. "It's a deal."

"Deal," she echoed.

～

"QUITTIN' time!" Miss Maple called.

Shannon glanced over and noted the older woman watching her from the doorway of her office. Miss Maple had her arms crossed over her chest as she leaned against the doorjamb. "But it's only four."

The older woman's hazel eyes gleamed with mischief as she said, "But you have a date tonight. Go on. Take your time getting ready. Pamper yourself. You deserve it."

Shannon rolled her eyes and continued restocking the front case with chocolate covered caramels. "It's a fake date with Brian. I hardly need to get all prettied up."

"You can't fool me, Shannon Ansell. I know how much you're looking forward to this. Stop acting cool. Not with me."

Her boss's words stopped Shannon in her tracks. Miss Maple was the one person in town Shannon trusted enough to actually confide in. And she was right, of course. Shannon was looking forward to the date. She was just trying not to think too hard about that inconvenient truth. "Okay. Fine. You win. I'm definitely not dreading this date. But that doesn't mean I need to leave work early. It won't take me that long to get ready. I'll be home by five-thirty. He is supposed to pick me up at six. That's just enough time to refresh my make-up and change clothes."

"Oh, honey." Miss Maple strode over to Shannon and nudged her aside. "Nope. I won't have my girl rushing tonight. Go home. Shave your legs. Pull on something that hugs those curves and will make him drool. Do it for me. It's been ten years since I had a hot date. Let me live vicariously. Okay?"

Shannon giggled at the earnest expression on Miss Maple's face. "You're pushing it. You know that, right?"

Miss Maple grinned and pointed to the door. "Go. I'll close up. But tomorrow I want all the sordid details."

"You're a piece of work," Shannon muttered even as she untied her apron and started striding toward the back room to grab her purse.

"You love me anyway," Miss Maple called after her.

Shannon couldn't argue with that. Ever since Shannon started working at A Spoonful of Magic a decade ago, Miss Maple had stepped in to take on the role of her family. She'd been there for Shannon when her mother had threatened to disown her, when her father had an affair with her mother's best friend and ended up in the tabloids, and when Shannon had broken her leg after tripping off the curb and had been laid up for weeks.

Miss Maple had been there for Shannon in a thousand

other small and large ways over the years. She'd even made Shannon the manager of A Spoonful of Magic, the store Miss Maple loved with her whole heart and soul. The fact that Miss Maple trusted Shannon meant the world to her. It was no exaggeration to say that Shannon more often thought of Miss Maple has her mother figure than she did the woman who'd birthed her.

After hanging up her apron, clocking out, and grabbing her handbag, Shannon went back into the front of the store to find her mentor. "Maple?"

"Over here, dear."

Shannon followed the sound of her voice out into the lobby where she spotted Miss Maple lying on the floor on her back as she studied the underside of one of the tables. "What are you doing?"

"Countering a love spell." Holding a neutralizing bottle and a white cloth, she reached up and sprayed the area before swiping at something on the underside of the table. "Earth magic. Very rudimentary. I'd guess a student did this."

"How?"

"It's a potion mixed with mud which means—"

"It would be tainted with other elements, causing the spell to go haywire," Shannon finished for her.

"Exactly. I hope whoever sat here last has some strong defense mechanisms, otherwise, someone's love life is about to go haywire," Miss Maple finished.

Shannon pursed her lips and tried to remember who'd been in the store that day. No one who'd spent any time at the few tables. It had been a slow day, and most had ordered their sweets and taken off in a hurry. That was probably because of the summer concert down by the river that day. "I wonder how long it's been there."

Miss Maple climbed back to her feet. "No more than a few days. As soon as I sat at the table, I felt the magic. It was faint but noticeable."

Shannon chewed on her bottom lip. It bothered her that she hadn't noticed the problem, though she readily acknowledged that Miss Maple's magic was far more powerful than her own. It wasn't a surprise that the older witch had felt it when she hadn't. "I'm sorry. I should make an effort to check the tables for stuff like that."

Miss Maple waved a hand. "You couldn't have known. It was subtle. Now go. Get ready for your date and don't worry about anything here. I've got it covered."

Shannon hesitated, not sure she should leave just yet, but when Miss Maple gave her a pointed stare and then gestured to the door, Shannon chuckled and did as she was told. She loved her boss and didn't want to insult her by not taking her up on her generous offer.

"See you tomorrow!" Shannon waved as she headed toward the door.

"Don't worry about being on time. I'll open," Miss Maple called back. "You just enjoy that date, no matter how long it lasts."

Shannon suppressed a groan and muttered, "This Cinderella turns into a pumpkin at midnight. Count on it."

CHAPTER 4

*S*hannon steered her little red Mustang down the tree-lined street, humming to herself. No matter what she'd told Miss Maple or Hope, she had to admit to herself that she was looking forward to whatever date Brian had planned. Even if she was determined to not fall for him, that didn't mean she didn't enjoy his company. She did. Very much so. If she didn't, she never would've agreed to the bet they'd made for six dates in six weeks. He made her laugh and feel good about herself. Pseudo-dating him wasn't exactly going to be a hardship. She just needed to figure out how to keep her heart out of the equation.

She whipped her car into the driveway and whistled to herself as she made her way up the flower lined path to the front door.

"Shan?" a familiar voice called from somewhere near her porch.

"Silas?" She whipped her head up and scanned the area, searching for her little brother. "Is that you?"

"It is." He stepped out of the shadows and held his arms open wide, waiting for her to reach him.

"Oh. Em. Gee! What are you doing here?" She ran to him and hugged him tightly. "Why didn't you tell me you were coming?"

He hugged her tighter and spun her around before he said, "Where's the fun in that?"

Shannon knew he was trying for a flippant, teasing tone, but his voice came out choked and full of something that sounded a lot like pain. "Silas?" She pulled back and took a good look at him. There were dark circles under his eyes and a worry line in his forehead. He was only a teenager. He shouldn't have to deal with worry lines for years to come. She pressed her thumb to the line above his brows and said, "What's got you worked up, little brother? You're only seventeen. Life can't be that rough, can it?"

Silas let out a humorless laugh. "Right. You do remember our parents, don't you?"

There was a hard edge in his tone she hadn't heard before that made her heart sink. She knew exactly what he was talking about, but she'd always hoped her parents had reserved their selfish demands for her and not Silas. He was, after all, the very reason those two had a career at all anymore. "Unfortunately." She gave him a sympathetic smile as she used her key to unlock her door. "Come on in and tell big sis all about it."

He followed her inside and straight to the back of the house to her sunny kitchen.

She pulled out a pitcher of iced tea and poured them both something to drink. "What is it? What did they do this time?"

Silas stared at his tea glass with one eyebrow raised. "Don't you have anything stronger?"

Shannon took in her brother's messy brown curls and weary dark eyes. He looked tired. Not just physically tired, but emotionally tired. "You know damned well I'm not going to serve you alcohol. I don't care what goes on down in Hollywood, you're still underage, and I—"

"Whoa there, Miss Goody-Two-Shoes," he said, rolling his eyes. "I meant something more like ginger beer or soda. You know, something with some flavor? Tea has never been my drink of choice."

"Yeah, okay. Nice save." Shannon retreated to the refrigerator, grabbed a ginger beer, and plunked it down in front of him. "This is one from the Townsend brewery."

"What? No cookies?" he asked as he sat down at the bar that separated the kitchen from the family room.

"You're pushing it, kid." Shannon knew he was stalling. Whatever was going on down in Hollywood, it had rattled her brother enough to send him all the way to Keating Hollow. She'd just have to let him tell her what was going on in his own time.

"Are you telling me there seriously aren't any cookies in your jar?" he asked.

She chuckled. "No. That's not what I'm saying. How do you feel about peanut butter cookies?"

"Lay them on me." He took a deep pull of his ginger beer but didn't take his eyes off her as she retrieved a handful of cookies from her *A Spoonful of Magic* cookie jar.

Once she placed them on a napkin in front of him, she got her own ginger beer and joined him. "It's damn good to see you, Silas. How long are you staying?"

"As long as you'll let me." He hunched forward, looking defeated as he stared down at his hands.

"Um, doesn't filming for your show start back up sometime

in the fall?" she asked gently. "Or are you thinking of leaving?" Silas was a series regular on a popular ensemble drama that revolved around a boarding school for paranormal beings. During the last few years, his star had risen, and Silas Ansell had practically become a household name.

"My contract isn't up until next year," he said and dropped his head to the counter.

Shannon placed a soft hand on his back. "What happened? Why do you want to leave?"

He heaved a heavy sigh. "It's not that I necessarily want to leave the show. I just don't want to be controlled by the parentals anymore." He raised his head and looked his sister straight in the eye. "They are trying to force me to do a reality show. One that follows me around and exposes my life to the entire world."

"What? You can't be serious." Shannon's eyes were wide, and she felt that familiar ache in her gut return. It was the one reserved just for their parents when they were being particularly heinous.

"Completely serious." He tightened his grip around the ginger beer bottle until his knuckles turned white. "They keep saying something about it coming with an endorsement deal that will triple my net worth and how this is going to turn me into the hottest star on the planet. But holy hell, Shan. There is no way I want cameras following me around. You know how private I am."

"Almost as private as me," she confirmed.

"Almost?" He let out a bark of laughter. "You're so private, you gave up Hollywood and the chance at an acting career to come back here and sell chocolate. I'd say you're ten times more private than I am."

"You might have a point." Shannon had run from

Hollywood when she was only twenty-one years old, right when her budding career had started to take off. She placed a soft hand over his. "Tell me what they did. What ultimatums did they give you?" If there was one thing she knew about her manipulative parents, it was that they'd do just about anything to get what they wanted. And if a reality show was going to triple Silas's net worth, that was a hell of a commission for her parents' management company.

He closed his eyes and squeezed them tight. His expression was so pained, and all she wanted to do was wrap him in her arms and keep him safe from the vultures until his eighteenth birthday. "Mom said if I didn't do it she'd tank all of the rest of my incoming offers and focus on Landon Perry instead. Apparently I'm ungrateful, and she won't waste her efforts on a spoiled-rotten kid who doesn't understand how to repay those who helped him get to the top."

"Ugh!" Shannon pressed her face into her hands and swallowed the primal scream threatening to break free. Their mother was the driving force behind the management company while their father golfed a lot and let her handle it all. There was a possibility he didn't even know what was going on with Silas. "And your money? Is she threatening to withhold that, too?"

"Of course she is. But that's nothing new. She threatens that at least once a day when I invariably do something she doesn't like. For instance, yesterday Mom was pissed I hung my towel up on the back of the bathroom door rather than the designated rack she'd had installed a month ago. And it wasn't even her bathroom. The woman is psycho."

"No argument there," Shannon said. Her mother had some really strange quirks. Some she could overlook, like her obsessive need to have everything in its perfect place. But the one that needed total control over her child's career despite his wishes? Nope. Not even close. "You should look into getting emancipated. You know that, right?"

"I know. I should have done it last year when she turned down the role in that independent film I wanted so much. She didn't even consult me before she had her assistant call and tell them thanks but no thanks. That script has stayed with me for months, Shan. Who wouldn't want to play a brilliant dancer who time travels to save his partner's life?"

"Mommy dearest? She'd only do it if the payday was at least six figures," Shannon said.

Silas snorted. "Please. She needs the offer to be *high* six figures, otherwise her cut isn't enough to bother with."

Shannon reached over and squeezed her brother's hand. "I'm so sorry, Si. I wish there was something more I could do."

"Letting me stay here is enough. LA was killing me. All I want to do is sleep and hike and pretend millions of people don't know my face."

"You got it, baby bro. How about a beach day later this week? Wednesday is my day off. We can get lost hiking in the redwoods for a while first."

Silas nodded. "Sounds perfect. But right now, I could use a shower. It was a long-ass drive to get here."

Shannon raised one eyebrow. "Where's your car? I didn't see it when I drove up."

He chuckled. "In the garage. It's a little too fancy for the folks around here. I didn't want to raise any suspicions."

"Too fancy? Did you trade in the starburst?" she asked, using his nickname for his lime green Toyota Prius.

"Mom did." He ground his teeth before adding, "She said it was better for my image if I had a sports car."

Closing her eyes, Shannon shook her head. It was hard to

believe they were related to the shallow woman who'd tried to live vicariously through both of them the last fourteen years. "That's ridiculous. I'm sorry, Silas. What did you end up with?"

"A Porsche. What else?"

"Only the best for Silas Ansell," Shannon mused, having trouble seeing her little brother whipping around in the high-performance car. The Prius had been perfect for him. If he'd wanted something fancier, a Tesla might be his speed. But a Porsche? Nope.

"That's right." He stood from his stool, waved a hand to unleash his air magic, and sent his ginger beer bottle to the sink. As he took off for the stairs, he asked, "I assume your guest room is free?"

"For you, always."

"Thanks, sis."

Shannon watched him disappear up the stairs, and while she was overjoyed that he'd come to stay with her, a ball of anger had taken up residence in her gut. She wondered what her dad had to say about the conflict between Silas and their mother. Likely nothing. The man was happy to sit back and let her steamroll both of their children just as long as his exclusive golf club memberships were paid and there was never any trouble getting a table at the fanciest restaurants. He didn't have the killer instinct that his wife did, but he very much enjoyed living the high life.

Lost in her thoughts about her parents, Shannon pulled her glitter-covered turquoise wand out of her purse and pointed it at her kitchen. Ingredients, along with a pot and baking pan, flew out of the cabinets as her magic went to work on making one of Silas's favorite meals. One she was certain he hadn't had since the last time he visited. Mac and cheese were not something television stars were allowed to indulge in. Not under the Ansell roof anyway.

Confident her magic would get the job done, she moved toward the living room at the front of her cottage and peered out just in time to see Levi start up the mower and get to work on her neglected yard.

"I feel so productive," she said, chuckling to herself. Between her magic and her delegation skills, she was downright domestic. Pleased with herself, she sat in her oversized armchair and took a well-deserved break.

She must have dozed off a bit, because what seemed like only a few moments later, she heard Silas say, "Who's the hottie mowing your yard?"

Shannon blinked her eyes open to find her brother standing in front of her picture window in clean jeans and a lavender button-down shirt. His hair was perfectly styled, and his skin glowed. He was beautiful and always had been. "Levi. He's Hope's half-brother. Just moved here a couple months ago."

"Hope?" he asked.

"Right. I haven't filled you in. She used to go by Luna. She's my new friend who works at the spa," Shannon said.

"Spa." A dreamy smile crossed his lips as he let out a sigh. "When's the soonest we can get an appointment?"

She laughed. "I'll call in the morning."

He turned and winked at her. "You're my number-one sister."

"I'm your only sister," she said, rolling her eyes. "Do me a favor?"

"What's that?" He was staring out the window again, forgoing any sort of subtlety as he watched Levi move across the yard.

"Get Levi something to drink while I finish up dinner." She hauled herself out of the chair and led the way to the kitchen.

"Dude. I'm totally on it." Silas strode past her into the kitchen and let out a gasp of surprise. "You're cooking mac and cheese?"

"Of course."

He turned around, threw his arms around her and said, "I love you."

"I know. Now get out of here so I can finish up."

Silas grabbed a couple more bottles of ginger beer from the fridge and disappeared out the front door while Shannon hummed to herself and set the table. Nothing made her heart fuller than having her brother back in town.

CHAPTER 5

*B*rian pulled his black SUV to a stop across the street from Shannon's small white cottage. Bright flowers lined her walkway and hung from the overhang on her porch. Her home was more welcoming and sweeter than he'd have imagined. She so often put on a hardened outer persona that she no doubt used to shield herself from the rest of the world. It made his insides warm to imagine being invited into the softer side of her life.

He slipped out of the vehicle and glanced over at the young man mowing her yard. He squinted, recognizing Levi Kelley, Hope Scott's brother. He was a good kid. Brian had gotten to know him a little since he'd been spending time at Chad Garber's music shop, teaching a few drumming lessons, so he wasn't surprised when Levi suddenly jerked his head up and stared right at him. The kid had spirit magic, which meant he could sense people who were in his vicinity without actually laying eyes on them.

Brian raised his hand to greet Levi. Levi smiled and waved back. A second later, Levi turned around abruptly when another kid strode out of the house carrying a couple of bottles. He moved across the porch and gestured for Levi to join him. Levi hesitated, but then he turned the mower off and moved toward the newcomer.

The dark-haired teenager looked vaguely familiar, but Brian couldn't place him. As far as he knew, Shannon didn't have any family in Keating Hollow. Was he a friend of Levi's? Whoever he was he had to be from out of town. Keating Hollow just wasn't big enough for everyone to not know everyone else.

"Hey, Brian," Levi called as Brian approached the porch.

"Hey, kid. How's the lawn care business going?" Brian asked.

"Excellent so far. Shannon is my first client." He turned to the other teenager, who was leaning against the railing. "This is Silas. Silas, meet Brian."

Brian held his hand out to the teenager. "Nice to meet you, Silas."

"You, too," the dark-haired kid said, shaking his hand. "Are you here for my sister?"

The front door flew open, and Shannon grimaced as she stammered, "Brian. Oh, man. I'm so sorry. I…" She glanced at Silas. "My brother surprised me. He's here from LA, and I should've called, but I don't think tonight is the best night. Can we reschedule?"

Disappointment weighed heavily on Brian's chest, but he nodded. What else was he going to do? Argue? Hardly. "Sure. It's—"

"Reschedule what?" Silas asked, his gaze shifting from Shannon to Brian.

"Nothing," Shannon said quickly. "It's not important."

"Ouch." Brian pressed a hand over his heart as if he'd been

wounded. "That hurts, Ansell. Not important? Kick a guy while he's down, why don't you."

"It's not nothing," Levi said helpfully. "Brian was supposed to take Shannon out on their first date."

Shannon raised her hand in a stop motion. "Wait just a—"

"A date?" Silas asked, gaping at his sister. "Why didn't you say something? You're not ready yet." Before she could say another word, he looped his arm through hers and tugged her toward the door. "Give us fifteen minutes, Brian. I'll have her whipped into shape."

"Silas!" Shannon hissed. "Stop. I'm a grown woman. I can deal with this myself."

"Apparently not," he shot back. "Otherwise you'd be in a sexy black dress, ready to paint this town red."

"Can you believe this?" Shannon asked as Silas ushered her into the house. "He's here for an hour, and suddenly he's running my life."

Brian grinned at Shannon and only shrugged. "It seems to be working in my favor, so I'm not complaining."

"Of course you aren't." She rolled her eyes and pressed one palm on the doorframe, planting her feet to keep herself in place. "Listen, I was in the middle of making dinner for Silas. It should be just about done. Think you can dish some up for both Silas and Levi while I get presentable?"

"Sure." He glanced at Silas, who was standing just inside the house, and gave the kid an appreciative nod.

"Let's go, Shan. Time to lose the boring shop-clerk outfit and get you into something date worthy." Silas winked at Brian and hauled her inside and up the stairs.

Brian turned to Levi. "Ready for some dinner?"

"I wasn't expecting Shannon to feed me," he said, eyeing the yard. "But I can't exactly say no since she cooked us something, now can I?"

"I couldn't," Brian confirmed.

"All right. Give me ten minutes to finish up and put my mower away."

Brian nodded and then strode into Shannon's house as if he owned the place. He could hear Prince's song "1999" playing from somewhere upstairs and wondered if that was from Shannon's or Silas's playlist. He assumed Shannon's since the song was older than both of them, but either way, he approved. Prince was one of the great musicians of their time.

Brian followed the rich cheese scent wafting through the house. It didn't take him long to find the kitchen, where utensils were flying around and chopping up vegetables for a salad, and a pitcher was hovering over a set of three glasses of ice, filling them each with water.

Three glasses.

That was surefire proof that Shannon had fully intended to blow him off, and he felt a wave of disappointment settle over him. He knew he'd messed up that night when he'd let things go too far, and Shannon had ended up in bed, beckoning to him, only for him to reject her. Was whatever was happening now supposed to be her revenge for being rejected?

He shook his head. Shannon was a lot more straightforward than that. No. She'd said her brother had surprised her, and he had no reason to not believe her. He glanced at the dining room table and thought, *What the hell?*

Twenty minutes later, when Shannon and Silas reappeared from upstairs, the table was set for four. He'd transferred the mac and cheese casserole to the center of the table and portioned the salad into matching bowls. A bottle of ginger beer had been placed in front of each plate along with the glasses of ice water.

"What's this?" Shannon asked, her eyes lighting up as she took in the spread. "Four? Are we staying in?" She glanced down at her shimmering silver dress that she'd paired with black leggings and chuckled. "I might be a little overdressed."

Brian stared at her, his mouth watering. The dress fit her in all the right places, showing just enough of her figure to make him want more, but not enough to be scandalous. She'd done something to her hair, making it smoother with big perfect curls that cascaded down her back, and she'd put on makeup that highlighted her perfect lips. All he wanted to do was stride over to her, wrap her in his arms, and kiss the hell out of her.

"Brian?" she asked with a laugh. "Are you okay?"

"Nope. He isn't," Silas said. "You're so hot right now you killed him dead. Poor guy can't even form words."

Levi snickered.

Silas winked at him, making the other boy blush furiously.

Brian cleared his throat and walked forward, offering her his hand. "You look stunning, Shannon."

She let out a nervous laugh. "I told Silas this dress was too much. Maybe I should change if we're staying in."

"Not on your life," Brian said, shaking his head. "Besides. We're not staying in. We're eating here and then I'm taking you both for a night out on the town."

"What?" Silas asked. "Who's both? You don't mean me, do you?"

"Sure." Brian glanced at her brother. "It's your first night here, right? I understand your sister wanting to spend time with you." He turned to Levi. "You're welcome to join us, too, of course."

Levi glanced down at his T-shirt and jeans and said, "Um, I'm not exactly cleaned up for a night out."

Silas eyed Levi and then Brian as he asked, "What exactly will we be doing? It's not like Keating Hollow is a mecca of nightlife."

"We'll be heading to the coast." Brian moved over to the table and pulled a chair out for Shannon. "Let's eat before it gets cold."

Her face lit up like Christmas, and Brian knew he'd just scored major points. Maybe she'd forgive him for their first date after all.

Shannon took her seat and eyed her brother. "Come on, Si. When's the last time you were out for a low-key evening without photographers everywhere?"

He shot Levi a worried look and then scowled at her. "Thanks for that. I was under the radar for what, like twenty minutes?"

Levi laughed. "Dude. I knew who you were the moment I saw you. It wasn't much of a stretch since you share a last name with Shannon."

"You did?" He frowned. "Why didn't you say anything?"

Levi shrugged. "I figured you must get a lot of people acting weird just because you're an actor. I never really did understand the whole celebrity-worship thing. You're still a person just like everyone else, right?"

A slow, easy smile slid over Silas's face as he nodded his appreciation. Then he turned his attention back to Shannon. "All right. I'll go if Levi does."

"Levi?" Shannon asked. "Care for a little adventure?"

"Sure, but do I have time to go home and clean up?"

"Brian?" Shannon asked. "Is whatever we're doing time sensitive?"

"Nope." He reached for the serving spoon of the mac and cheese and placed a mound of the pasta on her plate. "Not really."

"Don't worry about it. You can clean up here," Silas told him, eyeing the other teenager. "We look about the same size. I'll loan you something clean to wear."

"If you're sure," Levi said.

"I'm sure." He waited for Brian to release the serving spoon and then dished up mac and cheese for both himself and Levi.

"Thanks," Levi said, suddenly sounding shy.

"You're welcome, cutie." Silas turned his full attention to the other boy, pulling out all the charm that had made him famous.

Shannon snorted. "Subtle, Si."

He ignored her and continued to ask Levi about his life in Keating Hollow.

Brian wondered what Shannon would do if he started hitting on her as blatantly as Silas was hitting on Levi. She'd probably send him packing, he decided. He hadn't missed the fact that she seemed to be fed up with games and BS. If he wanted to win her over, he was going to have to work for it. But that was fine. He was more than up for the challenge.

CHAPTER 6

*S*hannon sat in the passenger seat of Brian's SUV, watching him steer the vehicle along the winding highway that led to the northern California coast. He wore a black button-down shirt with the sleeves rolled up to his elbows. She had a hard time tearing her gaze away from his forearms. His tanned skin and well-defined muscles were irresistible.

"Whatcha thinkin' about over there?" he asked in his slightly roughened voice.

"Huh?" She jerked her gaze from his arms to meet his eyes. Dammit. He was smiling at her knowingly as if he was well aware she'd been staring at him for the last five minutes.

"Care to share what's going on in that head of yours?" he asked with a teasing smile.

No. Never. He did not need to know she'd been wondering what it would be like to trail her fingers over his warm skin. Neither did the two teenagers in the back. Not that they were paying any attention to either Brian or Shannon. Levi was busy asking Silas about his life in Hollywood while Silas was more than happy to bask in the attention. Gods. If she didn't reign him in, his ego was going to be his downfall. Not that he was striking out with Levi. Quite the opposite actually. The two were getting along great. "Just wondering where you're taking us."

He chuckled. "Let's let that be a surprise."

Shannon rolled her eyes. As much as she wanted to tell him he was bombing this date and to get his G-string ready for when he was cleaning her pool, she really couldn't. The man had shown up for their date right on time. She was certain that he'd caught on to the fact that she was the one'd who'd forgotten that he was coming. And even then, he'd just rolled with it, stepping in to finish up dinner and even including her brother in whatever plan he'd concocted. If she was honest with herself, she had to admit that Levi wasn't the only one who was being charmed. Brian was scoring points all over the place. "Okay. But this better be good. I'd hate for you to have to stock up on sunscreen."

His eyes sparkled as he let out a laugh. "Don't get too attached to that fantasy. I have no intention of losing this bet. But if I do, don't worry about me. I've got the lotion covered."

Shannon's mouth went dry as she imagined running her hands all over him as she helped him protect his skin from the sun.

"Shan?" Silas asked.

"Yeah?" She turned around to look at her brother. "What's up?"

He glanced over at Brian and then back to her, his eyes slightly narrowed. "Care to share what this bet it?"

"Nope. It's not important," she said, pushing a red curl out of her eyes.

"Maybe not important, but it sounds really *interesting.*

Exactly where will Brian be using this sunscreen if he loses whatever bet you two have?" Silas asked.

"Never mind, little brother," Shannon said.

Brian snickered.

"And you," she said to her date. "Behave, or I'm going to ask you to take me home before this night even gets started."

"Oh, no you aren't. Levi and I did not spend all this time in the car just to head back to Keating Hollow. Did you forget that I just spent two days driving? We're going to have fun one way or another," Silas ordered.

Shannon suppressed a sigh. He was right. What she should've done was insist they stay in so that Silas could relax. Instead, she'd been excited that Brian had come up with alternate plans, because whether she wanted to admit it or not, she'd been looking forward to this date... even if she had forgotten all about it. *Guh.* She was the worst. Could she be any more hot-and-cold about this issue?

"Don't worry. I'll behave," Brian said, taking on a look that said he was all innocence.

She rolled her eyes again, but as she looked out the window at the blue water of the Pacific Ocean, she was smiling. The man just did something to her.

It wasn't long before Brian pulled into a parking lot full of cars. He killed the engine and hopped out, hurrying to open the door for Shannon. The two teenagers in the back were out of the car before she could even get her seatbelt unfastened.

Brian held his hand out to her, and warmth blossomed in her heart as he helped her out of his vehicle. It turned out chivalry wasn't dead after all.

"You've got to be kidding me," Silas said with a laugh. "Roller Palace? You brought us to a roller skating rink?"

Shannon turned and eyed the marquee over the front door

47

of the big boxy looking building. When she turned back to Brian, she raised her eyebrows. "Eureka has a roller rink?"

"Yep. Isn't it great?" He slipped his arm around her waist and started to guide her toward the entrance.

"Um, I'm not sure." She giggled as she caught the look on Silas's face. He wore an expression somewhere between surprise and horror. "Relax, little bro. This is going to be fun."

"Please tell me they have a skateboarding park out back," he said, shoving his hands into his front pockets.

"I doubt it," Brian said. "Besides, that would ruin the fun."

"How?" Silas asked.

"Because half the fun is the ridiculousness of the whole thing," Levi said, his eyes glinting with amusement. It was obvious he couldn't wait to see the famous television star rolling around a rink.

Silas turned his attention to Levi. Shannon wondered briefly if the Hollywood diva was going to rear his ugly head. It happened sometimes, and while it annoyed the crap out of her, she usually just called him out and then let it go. She understood that because their parents put him on a pedestal in order to get what they wanted out of him, he sometimes struggled to remain humble. But she needn't have worried. Silas gave Levi a genuine smile and said, "Yeah? You're down for some old-school skating?"

"I am if you are," he said.

Shannon shook her head as she watched them stride toward the entrance then she glanced up at Brian. "This wasn't the original plan, was it?"

He shook his head. "Nope. But it's inspired, don't you think?"

Chuckling, she leaned into him, nudging him playfully with

her shoulder. "I think it was risky. Looks like it's paying off though. How did you even know this place was here?"

"I overheard Candy talking about wanting to give it a try a few weeks back. I honestly didn't even think these places existed anymore. Last time I saw the inside of a roller rink, I think Hanson was still all the rage."

Shannon snorted, loving the image of him nodding his head along to "MMMBop." "Hanson? Really?"

Brian slipped his hand around hers and grinned. "Let's go find out what songs they play for the couples-only slow skate. What do you say?"

"I can hardly wait."

"Good." His dark eyes raked over her. "Just in case you were wondering, your skate card is full."

Tingles skittered over her skin. Gods, she loved it when he said things like that. She knew she should try to shake off the feeling. Falling for him wasn't an option, but dammit, he pushed all her buttons. Why couldn't she want someone less... dangerous to her heart?

Brian held the door open for her, and as they walked in, he pressed his hand to her lower back, keeping the connection that she knew she'd crave for days to come.

Levi and Silas had already paid for their admission, and once she and Brian were admitted into the facility, Shannon spotted her brother and Levi sitting on a bench, stuffing their feet into their rented skates.

"This should be interesting," Shannon said, feeling lighter than she had in weeks.

"Interesting? I'm shooting for fun." He sat down beside her and kicked off his shoes, showing her a more youthful side of him than she'd ever seen before.

"You're on."

The four of them spent the next two hours skating to the latest pop hits. When the couples skate came on, Brian led Shannon around the rink while Silas and Levi exited the floor to get some drinks. Shannon briefly wondered why Silas hadn't asked Levi to skate with him. The two seemed like they obviously liked each other, but perhaps her brother was just being his normal flirty self and didn't want to cause any expectations. Either way, she was glad they both appeared to be having fun.

As Shannon held hands with Brian and rolled around the rink, she smiled over at him. "Thank you for this."

"No need to thank me. I'm having a great time. Who knew listening to Taylor Swift while on a double date with your brother would be so fun?"

Shannon laughed. "I wouldn't call it a double date exactly. They just met."

Brian glanced over to where the two were sitting side by side at a table with their heads bent together as they talked. "If you say so, Shannon. But if that were my brother, I'd be having *the talk* with him later."

"*The talk?*" Her chest rumbled as she held back her laugh. "He's seventeen. Do you really think he hasn't had the talk before?"

"No idea." His expression turned sheepish. "But when I was seventeen, I could've used a weekly reminder."

She squeezed his hand, completely amused. "I bet. And your point is noted. I'll find out if the parentals did their birds-and-bees duty. And if not, I'll make sure he's covered."

Brian squinted as he studied the two boys. "Or a birds-and-birds conversation."

She was torn between rolling her eyes and chuckling again.

Instead, she shook her head, playfully admonishing him. "You did not just say that."

He smirked and turned around so that he was roller skating backward. But as he reached out to place his hands on her hips, one of his skates slipped out from underneath him and Brian went down in a tangle of limbs, taking Shannon with him.

"Oomph!" Shannon cried as she cracked her elbow on the hard surface. "Oh, ouch. Son of a... Damn, that hurts." She cradled her arm against her chest and felt the sting of tears burn her eyes.

"Oh, hell. Shannon, are you okay?" Brian scrambled onto his knees, reached for her upper arms, and carefully tugged her up with him. "Do we need to get you to a healer?"

"I, um... I'm not sure." Pain radiated from Shannon's elbow straight up to her shoulder, but she had no idea what kind of damage had been done. She wasn't ready to test it yet.

"Shannon?" Levi suddenly appeared over both of them, worry in his dark gaze. "That was a heck of a fall. Can you move your arm?"

"I don't know," she admitted. "I'm not sure I'm ready to try."

He nodded and held out a hand to Brian to help him up. Once her date was upright, he skated around behind her and then gently lifted her back onto her skates, careful to keep from getting anywhere near her elbow. "Let's get you off the rink."

Shannon nodded, feeling a little silly that Brian and Levi were hovering. She'd only smacked her elbow. It couldn't be anything serious, could it?

Once they were off the rink and seated at one of the many break tables, Brian went to work on getting her skates off while Levi stood next to her, gently rubbing his palms together. "Do you mind if I take a look at your arm?"

She blinked at the teenager. "Look at it how?"

"To see what kind of damage is there. I can't heal anything, but my spirit magic lets me sense things, and I should be able to determine if you need a healer. I've been working with Healer Snow a little bit. Hope takes me when she goes to help with other cases, and I'm learning how to better use my gift."

"Hope takes you?" Shannon asked, knowing the fact that Hope approved of his sessions with Healer Snow was the only reason she was considering letting a kid check to see if she'd cracked anything. While Hope was a massage therapist by trade, she also had special healing abilities and worked with Snow on hard to crack cases.

"Yes. She was anxious to have me start working with Snow. They both seem to think I'm useful." He shrugged one shoulder, clearly trying to show his humility.

"You sound damned useful, Levi." Shannon beckoned for him to stand right in front of her and added, "Okay, let's see if I have a broken wing."

Levi shifted so that he was standing behind her, and then started to gently massage her shoulders with wonderfully strong hands.

Warmth spread from his fingers down both arms, causing the burning pain to dull. After a moment, he slowly slid his hands down her arms, his touch barely a whisper against her skin. The pain didn't intensify, nor did it lessen more. It was just an annoying ache beneath the surface.

He let out a breath and let go. "Seems it's just going to be one heck of a bruise."

"So it's not broken?" Brian asked. His eyes were full of worry, and his body was tensed as if he was ready to jump into action.

Levi shook his head. "I really don't think so." He turned to face Shannon. "But a healer might put you more at ease and could probably make the pain go away."

"Nah." Shannon shook her head. Hope had told her a little about Levi's ability to sense things, and she trusted him. "I've got a pain killer potion at home. That should do the trick."

Brian's shoulders visibly eased, and he sat beside her, taking her hand in his. "Ready to go?"

"Probably," she said.

"We'll grab your shoes and drop off these skates," Silas said, nodding to Levi to join him on the mission.

After they were out of earshot, Shannon gave Brian a soft smile. "This was fun. Thanks."

"Despite the fact that I almost broke you?" he asked, one eyebrow raised.

"It was an accident." She leaned into him, gently nudging him with her shoulder. "Don't be so hard on yourself. Your clumsiness didn't ruin the date. You're still in the running to win the bet." She'd meant her words to be teasing, but when his eyes turned cloudy with an emotion she couldn't quite pinpoint, she frowned. "What?"

"I wasn't worried about the bet, Shannon. I just wanted to make sure this silly outing didn't end up with you in a cast."

Her insides turned to mush at his sincerity, and she tightened her fingers over his. "It wasn't a silly outing. I love that you included Silas and Levi last minute and that you chose something so... fun. Do you know the last time I was on a date that made me smile so much?"

"The last time I took you out?" he said with a cheeky grin.

She chuckled. "Cocky bastard. But no. That time I was too busy picturing what you'd look like naked."

That shut him up, ratcheting up her amusement. He blinked at her and then right before her eyes, his easy, humorous expression turned to one of pure heat. "Once we get you home, I can make sure you have an accurate picture to draw on next time you want to imagine me in all my glory."

"Uh, maybe another time," she said, patting his leg. "I've got a teenager who needs *the talk.*"

He groaned and pretended to be wounded by pressing a hand to his heart. "We'll need that second date ASAP."

"Six dates in six weeks, right?" she reminded him. "Does next Friday work for you?"

He shook his head. "No. I want to take you out tomorrow and the next night. And the night after that. What do you say? Change the terms? Six dates in six days?"

She knew he was teasing. His grin had widened, and his eyes were sparkling with mischief, but she also felt as if there were a sincerity hidden under what he wanted her to see. Gods. Her heart was going to burst right out of her chest if he kept that up. She wanted to challenge him, let him woo her for the next week. But as Silas returned with her high heels, she shook her head at Brian. "Nope. Next Friday."

Brian shrugged. "It was worth a try."

The ride home was full of easy chatter with the boys in the back talking about skateboarding, video games, movies, and planning a hike in the next few days. Shannon listened in, occasionally voicing an opinion or interjecting suggestions for things to do in the small town during the rest of the summer.

Brian was quiet, busy driving them back to town. He didn't speak until he pulled up in front of her house and the boys had already exited the SUV. "How's your elbow?"

"Not bad." She held her arm out and demonstrated bending it without wincing.

"Good." He got out of the car and came around to help her

out. After walking her to the door, he stood close, his hands resting lightly on her hips. "I had a really good time tonight."

She stared up into his dark eyes and nearly melted. There was a sweetness there she hadn't seen before. Was this the real Brian? Had she been wrong about him being a playboy from southern California? An image of Skye, the child he'd thought he'd fathered before he discovered she belonged to Jacob, flashed in her mind, and she reminded herself that it was possible to be sweet *and* be a playboy. Letting herself fall for this man was probably trouble waiting to happen.

Right?

"Shannon?" he asked, leaning in closer.

She swallowed thickly. "Yes?"

His tongue darted out to gently lick his lips, and his voice was hoarse when he asked, "Can I kiss you goodnight?"

There wasn't anything on the goddess's green earth that could make her refuse him in that moment. She stared up into his gorgeous dark eyes and said, "Yes."

CHAPTER 7

*B*rian sat in his SUV in front of his house and took a deep breath. What exactly had happened to him that night? He'd started off the evening hoping to crack a little bit of the shell Shannon had erected around herself. Get her to give him a chance, maybe start dating for real. Perhaps move their relationship into the territory of something more than friends.

Instead, he'd cracked his own shell. No, not cracked. Shattered. The overwhelming protectiveness he'd experienced when she'd gone down on her elbow had been unlike anything he'd felt for anyone before. He'd wanted to wrap her up in his arms, take her home, and take care of her for as long as she'd let him. In the end, he'd taken her home, kissed her goodnight, and drove home alone… like always.

Damn.

He'd never had a problem being alone before. In fact, he usually preferred it. Whatever he was feeling for Shannon was completely new, and he wasn't sure he was comfortable with it.

Light flooded his front porch, startling him. Who the hell

was in his house? He immediately reached for his phone, quickly scrolling through for Drew Baker, Keating Hollow's deputy sheriff. He'd already hit Call when the intruder came into view.

"Cara?" he said, although there was no way she could hear him as he was still in his SUV.

"Baker," Drew said on the other end of the line.

"Hey, Drew. It's Brian Knox. I thought I had an intruder, but it turns out it's a friend I wasn't expecting. Sorry to bother you over nothing."

Drew let out a small chuckle. "No worries man. I'd rather it be a false alarm than something serious."

"I hear you. See you tomorrow at the brew pub?

"Definitely. Have a good night." Drew ended the call while Brian pushed his door open.

"There you are," Cara said, her hands on her hips as she glared at him. "Where the heck have you been?"

Standing in his driveway, he narrowed his eyes at her and ignored her question. It was none of her damned business. "Cara. I thought you left for LA hours ago."

"I can see that." Her tone was just as icy as the expression on her face. "You were with *her*, weren't you?"

"If you mean Shannon, then yes, I was. What's it to you?" He moved past her and strode into his house, wondering how she'd gotten in. He distinctly remembered locking the door when he'd left earlier in the evening.

"We're dating!" she cried out from behind him, still standing on the porch.

Brian spun around so fast it wouldn't have surprised him to find he'd left a burn mark in the floor from his heel. "What?"

"We're dating. Our families are expecting an engagement by the end of the year." She threw her hands up and stalked past him into the kitchen where she pulled a bottle of wine out of the refrigerator and poured herself a glass.

Brian stood still, watching her in shock as she downed half the glass of white wine. Then the shock started to wear off as pure anger settled in. "We are *not* dating." She opened her mouth to protest but he put a hand up, stopping her. "I don't care what your father says. I took you to the wedding as a friend so you wouldn't have to go alone." His voice was harsh, even to his own ears, and he winced. Trying to be a gentleman and not a completely insensitive jerk, he softened his tone. "Listen, I'm sorry if you got the wrong impression, but I really don't think it's a good idea if we date."

"Because you want to get into Shannon's pants," she said, sounding petulant.

He couldn't exactly deny her claim. He did want Shannon. He wanted her more than maybe anyone, ever. But that was none of her business. And frankly, he resented her bringing it up. "Let's not go there, all right? Do you want to tell me why you turned around and came back to Keating Hollow?"

She crossed her arms over her chest and pressed her lips together.

He stared her down. "If you don't want to talk about why you're here, maybe you can tell me how you got in. My house was locked."

Her expression was sheepish as she turned away from him and mumbled something.

"What was that?" he demanded.

She threw her hands up. "I wiggled a window open. Go ahead. Have me arrested. I needed to use the restroom and couldn't wait any longer."

Cara looked ridiculous with her chin jutted out and her wrists together as if she was waiting to be cuffed. Suddenly

Brian was exhausted, and without another word, he turned and retreated deeper into his house.

Footsteps sounded behind him, and he suppressed a sigh. It wasn't as if he could just order her to leave. It was late, and she didn't have a car. He vaguely wondered how she'd gotten back to his house. Uber? A taxi? Probably one of the two. Or a hired car even. It didn't matter how. All he knew was that he had to offer her the guest bedroom again.

"I'm headed to bed," he said without looking at her. "The guest room is yours."

"I didn't eat dinner," she said.

He gritted his teeth, took a deep breath, and forced out, "Help yourself to anything in the fridge."

"Thanks." Her voice was small now, making him feel like a grade A jerk. But hell, he wasn't the one who broke into someone's house and accused them of cheating when they didn't even have a relationship.

He paused, running a hand through his hair. Turning, he met her wary gaze. "We'll talk in the morning after we've gotten some sleep."

"I think that's probably best," she said.

"Goodnight, Cara."

"Goodnight, Brian."

THE LOUD RING of Brian's business phone woke him from a deep sleep. He sat straight up in bed, blinking his blurry eyes. The clock read 7:07 am.

"Damn it all to hell," he muttered. "Who is calling at the butt crack of dawn?" Brian slid out of his bed clad only in his boxer briefs and headed out into the living room where his desk sat against one wall. Since he lived alone, he'd set up his work space in the spot with the best view of the valley below his two acres of property on the side of Keating Hollow mountain.

The phone continued to ring, disturbing his normally peaceful morning.

"Knox Designs," he said into the receiver.

"Knox. What the hell did you do to my daughter?" Manchester barked over the line.

Brian took a moment to process what his client had said. Then he cleared his throat. "I'm sorry, sir. I don't know what you're talking about."

"Don't be dense, Knox. You can't go around dating other women right in front of her. She's devastated. She called me before sunrise on the verge of tears. I'm going to need you to get on the first flight down here and apologize otherwise this business deal is going to go south fast."

"Um, what?" Brian walked quickly down the hall and peeked into the spare room. The bed was made, and Cara was nowhere to be found.

"You heard me. I can't work with the man who broke my little girl's heart. Get here by this evening or else I'm afraid I'll have to find another designer."

"I didn't—"

There was a loud click on the other end. The bastard had once again hung up on him. Brian slammed the phone down and called, "Cara? Are you here?"

Silence.

Brian breathed a sigh of relief. Had she left? He could only be so lucky. After pulling on a T-shirt and a pair of jeans, Brian made his way to his kitchen and tasked himself with making coffee. After he had a hit of caffeine, then he'd start dealing with the morning. But as the coffee started to brew, he spotted a note sitting on the bar area. Reluctantly, he picked it up and read the neat scrawl.

Brian,

I think we need a break so that each of us can figure out what we want from this relationship. I've headed home on the 6 am flight. Call me once you've decided to do the right thing for all of us.

Cara.

She'd drawn a tiny heart next to her name that made him want to vomit. Instead, he crumpled up the note and tossed it in the garbage. How had he ended up in this twilight zone? He'd never dated Cara. He'd never agreed to date Cara. Well, not really, anyway. He'd taken her on a couple of dates when they were teenagers, but that had been more than fifteen years ago. Even then their parents had hinted that when the time was right, the pair would get married. Brian had always ignored them. Because who thinks about getting married at nineteen? Certainly not him and not to someone who his parents picked out for him.

With his coffee in hand, he moved back to his desk, glanced down at the sketches he'd made for Manchester, and then promptly slid the entire folder into the trash. There weren't any circumstances that could get him to design the plans for Manchester's new spa now. Not after the old man had threatened him.

The phone started to ring again. He let out a curse and picked it up. "Knox."

"Brian," his father's voice boomed over the phone.

"Were you expecting someone else?" He took a sip of his coffee and sat in his leather office chair.

"Don't be flippant. What did you do to Cara Manchester? Her old man just called and gave me an earful. He's threatening to pull out of our partnership if you don't clean up your mess."

"Then you're going to have to find a new partner, Dad, because that man is batshit crazy. I didn't do anything to his daughter." Brian reached over and flipped on his desktop computer.

"He said you broke her heart. Fix it," his father growled.

"No."

"No?" his father asked in a mocking tone, as if it was ludicrous for Brian to defy him. And maybe it always had been in the past, but not anymore. Brian didn't work for the family business, nor did he ever intend to. Not again. And even if his design business never took off, that was fine. He owned an extremely profitable online spa supply business that had nothing to do with the Knox Corporation. When Brian didn't say anything, his father added, "You will smooth things over with Manchester and Cara, or there *will* be consequences."

"What consequences, Dad? You'll cut me out of the will? News flash; I don't care. Do what you need to do. But no one is going to dictate who I date or marry. I will not be a stud pony for you, not for the Knox Corp, and not to further my own business interests. Got it?"

His father let out a sigh that sounded more tired than annoyed. "Of course you shouldn't do that. I would never suggest you compromise your integrity, but if we don't do something, a major deal is going to blow up in our faces."

"Our faces, Dad? I'm not a part of Knox Corp anymore. What exactly do you expect me to do? Pretend to be interested in Cara just so you can get what you want out of this deal? Well, I've got news for you. That isn't going to happen. I'm dating someone. In fact, I'm bringing her to Brittany's wedding. You can meet her then."

There was a long pause before his father asked, "How serious is it?"

"As serious as it gets," he said and felt his heart skip a beat. Damn. He had to get that under control, didn't he? He'd always intended to take Shannon to the wedding and introduce her as his fiancée. It was a self-preservation move and part of the bet. He hadn't expected to like the idea as much as he did.

"Did you get her a ring?" His father was all business now. No doubt he wanted to know exactly what type of woman he was getting for a daughter-in-law. Well, he could keep wondering. He had no intention of spilling more details about Shannon until they showed up at his sister's wedding.

"No. But I plan to." Brian was surprised to find the idea didn't panic him like it might have a year before. Had time mellowed him or was it just that he was picturing a different woman by his side? He shook his head. None of this was reality. It was just a story to get his family off his back. He needed to stop picturing Shannon with a rock on her finger.

"I see. Well hold off on that thought for a bit. I think there is a way to salvage this deal without marrying you off to the Manchesters. But I'm going to need your help."

"Doing what?" Brian asked, pressing a hand to his forehead. Why was he part of this family? There was a reason he'd moved five hundred miles away from them.

"We need to talk Manchester down, but he isn't going to be receptive if you're flaunting a fiancée. Can you get here this afternoon?"

No. The real answer was yes, he could. But there was nothing short of a medical emergency that was going to get him down to southern California after the ultimatum Manchester had given him. He recapped the conversation for his father and said, "I don't think either of us want to let Manchester feel like he's in a power position. If I go down there, he'll think he calls all the shots."

"Right." His father sucked in a sharp breath. "Okay. Never mind. I'll deal with him. Just... for now, keep a low profile."

"Don't I always?" Brian asked. "No one is writing society gossip pieces about me up here."

"No, but if anyone finds out Manchester was expecting an engagement that isn't coming, don't think being in Keating Hollow is going to give you any cover. The vultures will be circling."

That was fair enough. The Knox name was well known enough that if the gossip rags caught wind of something, they'd swoop in like seagulls on a lobster dock. No thanks. He loved his quiet life in Keating Hollow. He didn't need any reporters to mess it up. "Got it. I'll talk to you later. I need to get to work."

"Do you even have any?" his father asked. "I heard Manchester pulled the plug with you."

Brian rolled his eyes. "Yes, Dad. I have a thriving online supply business, remember? There's always something to deal with. Honestly, I don't care about Manchester's design. Now I'm free to find other clients and not be locked in with his no compete clause. The man was horrible on all levels."

"Is that so?" his father asked.

"Yep. Just be careful what you concede to him. He'll exploit it all. Trust me. Make sure your contracts are tight."

"They always are."

CHAPTER 8

*T*he sweet scent of caramel and chocolate filled the air as Shannon opened the display case to clean the shelves. She hadn't had a break all day at A Spoonful of Magic and couldn't wait to get home to put her feet up.

It was late in the afternoon, about twenty minutes before closing when exhaustion settled over Shannon's weary limbs. After her night out at the skating rink with Brian and the two teenagers, she'd said goodnight to Levi and Silas, leaving them in front of the television, and had gone straight to bed. Unfortunately, she hadn't done much sleeping. In fact, she'd lain in her bed reliving the kiss Brian had given her, wishing she'd had the nerve to invite him inside. Instead, she'd kissed him one last time, told him she had a great time, and then hurried inside before she caved. Asking him to stay was a mistake she wasn't going to make again.

Considering how tired she was, she was once again grateful for her air magic. It allowed her to wave her wand and send the mop around the confectionary shop floor, saving her the physical effort. Just ten more minutes and she'd be free to go home, curl up in her yoga pants, and eat leftover mac and cheese. She couldn't wait.

The mop had just about finished its job when the phone started to jingle like a set of bells. Miss Maple told her once that if they had to have a phone, the ring could at least be pleasant. Shannon agreed, but today she was just irritated that someone was calling five minutes before closing.

Pasting on a smile that she hoped would force a cheery tone, she answered, "A Spoonful of Magic, how can we charm your day today?"

"Shannon?" Her mother's voice was harsh as she barked into the phone. "Where the hell is Silas? We have a meeting tomorrow morning that he can't miss."

Shannon bit back her groan while trying to ignore the sinking feeling in the pit of her stomach. "Good afternoon, Mother. It's been a while, hasn't it? How are you?"

"Not great. Where's your brother. He is with you, isn't he?"

The desire to just hang up and pretend the phone call had never happened was strong. But Shannon couldn't do that. Silas was, after all, still a minor, and although Shannon disagreed with just about every decision her parents made when it came to Silas and what was best for him, they at least deserved to know he was safe. "Yes. He's here in Keating Hollow, but he's not here with me at work. He's probably at home or out hiking or something."

"Hiking! He can't do that. His new show starts filming next week. If he hurts himself, that's going to be a huge problem. I need you to find him and make sure he's on the next plane to Los Angeles. Text me his flight information, and I'll have a car waiting for him."

The bells over the door of the shop chimed, and Shannon glanced up to find Silas and Brian both walking through the door. Silas had a smirk on his face while Brian was holding a bouquet of sunflowers. Brian mouthed, *Hi*, and sent her a sexy grin that sent a bolt of pleasure through her.

Whoa. Where was the fan when she needed one?

"Shannon? Did you hear me?" Gigi Ansell asked.

"I heard you. But he's not going to get on a plane, Mom. His car his here, and as far as I can tell, he doesn't want to do this new show. Didn't he tell you that?"

"Mom?" Silas whispered and turned pale as he scowled.

Shannon nodded, sending him a sympathetic look.

"Pfft. We'll hire someone to drive it back. Or you can do it. It's been far too long since you've been home to see us. I swear, that sleepy town is like quicksand and has swallowed you whole. You need to get out of there before you can't remember how to interact with the rest of the world."

"I'm not driving down to LA." The last time she'd left, she'd vowed to never go back. Her parents had ruined it for her.

"Fine. Get on a plane with Silas then. It's not a problem to hire a driver. I'll expect you both tomorrow."

"That's just not possible. I have a job here. I can't pick up and do whatever you ask at a moment's notice," Shannon said, holding her emotions back. If she didn't, she'd be screaming into the phone.

"How many times have I told you that you don't need to work at that ridiculous little shop?" Gigi said, her disapproval coming through loud and clear. "There is a job waiting for you at the management company until we can get your portfolio back into shape. You just need to—"

"Mother, I don't need to do anything. I like it here. I'm happy here. It can't be that bad. You raised me here." The Ansell's had moved to Keating Hollow when Shannon was just seven years old. Her dad's mother had lived there, and he'd convinced Gigi they needed to take care of his mother in her golden years. Gigi had gone along with it grudgingly. She'd had big plans of breaking into Hollywood. She'd had a few minor roles, but nothing that paid the bills. So when money was tight and Grandma Ansell needed a caretaker, the three of them moved.

Eleven years later, when Silas was only four years old, Grandma Ansell had passed, and Shannon was entering UCLA, the entire family moved to southern California. Gigi was intent on turning Shannon and Silas into stars. Four years later, Shannon had graduated from college and immediately moved back to Keating Hollow. She was done with call backs, being told she needed to lose ten more pounds, and most of all, answering to her critical mother. Her only regret was leaving Silas alone with them.

That was when Gigi Ansell had turned her entire focus on Silas. In the past nine years, he'd modeled for more catalogs and appeared in more commercials than she could count. But unlike Shannon, he actually liked the work. It was too bad their mother was doing her best to ruin his love for the business.

"I was forced to move to Keating Hollow. You know that. Your father... Well, he's always gotten his way when it's come to our marriage, but ever since he slept with *that* woman, things have changed. I call the shots now. In fact, he's out schmoozing the execs from Stream Box. It's a new streaming service, and I'd bet my new Louboutins that I could get you signed on as part of the ensemble cast in their new show that's coming out next year. What do you say? Should I set up a meeting for tomorrow afternoon?"

Betting her Louboutins would mean she was more than a hundred percent certain she could get what she wanted. If there was one thing her mother really cared about, it was her designer shoes. Status was everything to her.

"No thanks," Shannon said, pretending it was no big deal that she was casually turning down a meeting with an exec big wig. In fact, it wasn't to her. She'd liked acting, but didn't care for the business end. And if it meant her mother managing her career, that was a hard pass. "I'll be here in Keating Hollow with Silas. I think you need to give him a break. He's burned out, Mom. Let him rest a few days and then give him a call."

"Rest? He's been off for over a week already." Gigi scoffed. "He's seventeen, not forty-seven. All he needs to do is sleep in one day and he'll be as good as new."

"Um, have you noticed him lately? He has bags under his eyes and is much paler than normal. I think the best thing you can do is give him a break," Shannon said.

"Gee, thanks, sis. Good to know you think I look like death," Silas muttered.

Shannon pressed her palm to the receiver and whispered, "Shh, I'm buying you a few days before you need to deal with her."

He raised his hands in a surrender motion and then sat down, sprawling out in one of the chairs.

Her mother let out a very put-upon sigh. "Fine. But if he doesn't answer when I call two days from now, I'm going to fly up there and bring him home myself."

"Mom, I don't—"

"Forget it, Shannon. This isn't a game. It's his entire career. If he needs to play in the redwoods for a few days, then fine. But I'm not going to let him hide out for the rest of the summer. He has commitments to deal with."

There was a distinct click, and Shannon knew her mother had ended the call. She replaced the receiver onto the store's landline and walked over to the table to take a seat next to Silas.

"Well?" he asked.

Shannon rubbed at her temple. "I got you two days before her head explodes. She's demanding that you talk to her then or she'll come up here and get you herself."

He groaned and covered his face with his hands.

"I'm sorry. Did you go see Lorna White today?" she asked, referring to the town's attorney.

"No." He dropped his head onto the table and started to gently knock his skull against the wood.

"Don't knock something loose," Brian said with a slight chuckle. "I bet she's still at her office if you want to go now."

He stopped his self-destruction and turned his head to look at Shannon. "Do you think I can trust her?"

"Probably," Shannon said. "Lorna is a small-town lawyer who doesn't give a crap about prestige or pissing off the wrong person. In other words, Mom won't have any influence over her, unlike some of the lawyers in Hollywood."

"Ugh. Fine." He pushed himself up to his feet. "I'll go talk to her."

"Do you want some company?" Shannon asked as she stood. She was dying to go with him, to hear with her own ears what Lorna might have to say, but she also knew Silas was tired of being handled. Some things he needed to deal with himself.

"No. Not tonight. I just want to find out what's involved and how long it will take. If it's a six-month process, it's hardly worth it, right?" he asked.

"Right." He'd be eighteen in just eight months. Anything that could drag on probably wasn't worth the family drama.

"I'll see you back at home." He moved to the front door, but just before he left, he turned to Brian and said, "Good luck, man."

Shannon raised an eyebrow at Brian. "What do you need luck for?"

"This." He handed her the bouquet of sunflowers, reached into a canvas bag she hadn't noticed before, and pulled out a candle. After lighting it with just his thumb and forefinger, he placed it on the table and stepped back, circling his arm around Shannon's waist.

"Impressive," she teased, referring to the minor display of his fire magic.

He grinned down at her. "Wait for it."

Shannon eyed him suspiciously. "What's—"

The flame shot up into the air and morphed into a sparkling wand. The wand scribbled through the air, leaving behind the words, *Will you have dinner with me?*

Shannon couldn't help but be charmed. How cute was that?

"If you're not up for dinner, I'll be content with a drink or a walk down by the river. I just wanted a moment alone with you since our date ended up including teenagers. Not that I didn't enjoy them. Both Levi and Silas are good kids."

"They are." Shannon said, casting him a sidelong glance. "Does this count as date number two?"

She could see him mentally weighing how he wanted to answer her question. If he said yes, it would significantly up the chance she'd say yes. If he said no, he'd still have five more dates and plenty of time to plan them before the bet was over. "You told me yesterday the bet was for one date a week for six weeks, so no. This one doesn't count. I'd just like to spend some time with you and get to know you a little better before the next date."

Hell, how could she say no to that? The fact was she didn't

want to say no. And after dealing with her nightmare of a mother, all she wanted was to put the conversation out of her mind. Brian was the perfect distraction. "Okay, sure. How about dinner at the pub and then a walk down by the river?"

His lips split into a wide grin. "You don't have to ask me twice." He held his arm out to her. "Ready?"

"Definitely." She pulled her wand out of the holder at her waist, flicked the tip and sent the mop bucket back to its place in the still-open closet, and then reached over and turned out the lights before stepping out onto the cobbled sidewalk of Keating Hollow's Main Street.

CHAPTER 9

*B*rian slipped his hand into Shannon's and ignored the strange pressure in his chest that had materialized the moment she'd agreed to the date. He'd fully expected her to say no, especially after he'd tried to impress her with his cheesy magic trick. He let out a small chuckle, both embarrassed and amused at his amateur dating moves.

"What's so funny?" Shannon asked. The sun was low in the sky, providing a warm glow that gave her features a luminosity in the late afternoon light.

"Me. I can't believe my fire trick actually worked." He felt his face get hot and willed the flush to go away.

Shannon laughed. "Okay, it was a little cheesy. But I like that. Anyone who can make me laugh gets bonus points."

"Is that why you said yes? You find me amusing?"

"Yes… and no." She shrugged one shoulder. "Honestly, I wanted a distraction from dealing with my mother. She always has a way of getting under my skin."

Brian let out a snort. "That sounds exactly like my

relationship with my father. I also had one of those conversations today."

They shared a long glance, both of them silently commiserating with the other.

He tugged her a little closer, steering her away from the sticky mess of a melted ice cream cone that had been left in front of Incantation Café.

She glanced down at the sidewalk, and when she looked back up, there was a tender expression in her eyes. "Thanks."

"Don't mention it." He loved that he'd managed to work past her sassy outer layer to find her softer side. It made him want to do it again and again.

The Keating Hollow Brewery was surprisingly quiet despite the fact that it was summer, a notoriously busy time of year for the town. Sadie, a petite blonde, rushed over to greet them. "Hey Shannon, Brian. Just the two of you tonight?" she asked.

"Yep." Brian dropped Shannon's hand and placed his on the small of her back.

"What's going on? Where is everyone?" Shannon asked as they followed Sadie to a table near the window.

"There's some sort of tasting party over at the Pelshes' that Rex Holiday put together. Free wine does the trick every time." She smiled. "But you know what? Even though my tips are going to suck tonight, I don't really mind. It's nice to have a break every once in a while."

"I hear you," Shannon said. "No wonder the shop was slow this afternoon."

"Yeah." Sadie nodded. "I think Rex is trying to gauge audience reactions to the wines he's been working on with Mr. Pelsh. They're testing their early blends and trying to decide which ones to put into production and which ones they want to age longer. I heard Mr. Pelsh also has some from last year that he bottled that they are going to try. It sounds like quite the community party if you ask me."

"It sure does," Brian said, taking a menu from her. "But tonight I think I'll just have Rhys's new pear cider. I hear it's really good."

"I want to try the apple," Shannon said. Rhys was the brewery's assistant manager and had recently been put in charge of producing ciders.

After assuring them she'd be right back with their drinks, Sadie took off for the bar.

"Isn't Rex a friend of yours?" Shannon asked.

Brian frowned. "He was until he started putting the moves on my girl at Jacob's wedding reception."

Shannon let out a bark of laughter. "Your girl?"

He nodded. "Bro code means hands off."

"Bro code?" She scoffed. "You can't be serious."

"I'm dead serious. He already knew I had my eye on you. The fact that he put his hands all over you is a major foul. It might mean the end of a friendship that has lasted over a decade."

Shannon rolled her eyes. "We were dancing, not making out. And if you end your friendship over that, then you're an idiot."

"I am? Why?" he asked, eyeing her carefully. A rumble of laughter was starting to build in his chest at the rise he was getting out of her. His friendship with Rex wasn't in any danger. In fact, he knew Rex had asked her to dance just to get under Brian's skin. It had been a dare of sorts.

"Because you just are," she said, sounding exasperated. "I'm not at the winery, am I? I didn't even know about the event. Instead I'm here with you. That should tell you something."

A slow smile spread across his face. She was right. It told him everything he needed to know.

An hour later, Brian paid the bill, stood, and held his hand out to her. "Ready for that walk?"

"I'm going to need it after mac and cheese last night and the burger and fries tonight. Jeez. I feel like I've gained ten pounds in two days.

He let his gaze roam over her, loving every inch of her curvy figure. "Not possible. But if you did, I'd say it went to all the right places."

Shannon gave him a look that said he'd lost his mind.

He just laughed and tugged her out of the brewery. The air had turned slightly chilled, and when he noticed gooseflesh pop out on her bare arms, he steered them back to his SUV that was parked in front of Chad's music store.

"Are we driving somewhere?" Shannon asked with a small frown.

"No. You look chilled." He opened the back door behind the passenger seat and pulled out a gray zip-up sweatshirt. "I thought you might need this."

And there was that expression again. The tender one that made him feel as if he could see right into her soul. Damn if that look wasn't going to be the end of him one of these days.

"Thank you," she said, slipping it on. The sweatshirt was at least two sizes too big for her, but Brian loved that. There was nothing sexier than seeing the girl you're crushing on wearing your clothes. It was as if he'd claimed her as his by loaning her a piece of his clothing.

Get a grip, Knox. You're not in high school, you poor bastard, he told himself. He stifled a chuckle and slipped an arm around her waist, pulling her to his side.

"You're laughing again. What is it this time?" she asked as

they started to make their way down the street toward the river.

"I'm not laughing," he lied. "I'm just enjoying an evening walk with my future fiancée." He winked at her, and she blushed. Damn, he liked that.

"Fake fiancée," she corrected. "And don't get presumptuous. You might've started off strong, but who's to say you won't have a weak finish?"

Brian stopped in his tracks and stared down at her, both eyebrows raised. "Weak finish? Are you kidding me? I'm a closer. I always get the job done." His voice had gone smoky, and there was no hiding the desire there. He reached up and brushed a lock of hair out of her eyes as he added, "Trust me on this one."

Shannon licked her lips just as she dropped her gaze to his mouth.

Hell. She was going to kill him, wasn't she? "Shannon, if you keep looking at me like that, I'm going to kiss the ever-loving hell out of you."

"Okay," she breathed.

That was it. He was done. There was no holding back. She'd given him the go-ahead, and nothing on earth was going to stop him now. He pressed both of his palms to her cheeks and leaned in until his lips were barely an inch from hers. But as much as he wanted her, he needed to be certain she was just as into this as he was. "You're sure?"

Shannon reached out, grabbed his shirt with her fist, yanked him the rest of the way so that their bodies were pressed together, and answered by covering his mouth with hers.

His hands immediately slipped into her hair as he tilted her head to the side for easier access. The kiss was hot and hungry.

They'd been doing this ritual dance for months, and now it was as if they were both starving.

Shannon let go of his shirt, slipped her arms around his waist, and started to glide her fingers up and down his back. Her touch was heaven, but not nearly as magical as her mouth. Gods, he loved the way she tasted of salt and cider and something slightly sweet.

"You taste like sugar cookies," she murmured against his lips.

He pulled back and chuckled. "What? How is that possible?"

She shrugged. "I don't know, but I freakin' love sugar cookies."

In the next instant, her lips were on his again. By the time they pulled apart, they were both breathing heavily. Brian pressed his forehead to hers and whispered, "Do you have any idea how much I want to take you home right now?"

She let out a slow breath. "About as much as I want to take you home."

Brian let out a low growl. "Dammit, Shannon. Don't say things like that unless you mean it."

"Oh, I mean it." But even as she said the words, she pulled back and bit her bottom lip. "The problem is I need to get home and talk to Silas. He's going to need to talk to me about the lawyer."

"Right." Brian closed his eyes, trying to will his body to calm down. "Of course you do. Can I walk you home or did you drive to work?"

"I walked, but I thought we were headed to the river," she said.

"Shannon, if I take you down to the river, I'm ninety-five percent sure I'm going to try to get you naked under one of the trees. As much as I would love to spend some more time with you, it might be best if we call it a night."

She threw her head back and laughed.

"Oh, like you wouldn't be thinking about it?" He eyed her, all but challenging her to deny his claim.

"You're right. I would be. I just find it extremely amusing that you're so open about it. I like that." She pressed up onto her tiptoes and brushed her lips over his one last time. "It's part of the reason why I like you so much. I love that you don't hold your thoughts back... Well, you usually don't."

Her expression had turned rueful, and he was certain he knew exactly what she was talking about. The memory of the night when he'd walked out on her flashed in his mind, and the image was so vivid it made him take a step back and run a hand down his face.

"Do you think you'll ever tell me what really happened that night?" she asked.

He jerked his head back up, surprised she'd been so blunt about it. Though he shouldn't have been. That was just Shannon's personality and one of the reasons he found her so attractive. "Yeah. I'll tell you on the way back to your house."

CHAPTER 10

Shannon was quiet as she walked side by side with Brian down Main Street. She desperately wanted to hear why he'd rejected her that night, but she also suspected it was something deeply personal that he wasn't comfortable talking about. It was better to let him find his way into the conversation rather than push it. He'd already said he'd tell her. She just needed to wait him out.

They'd gone quite a few blocks and had just turned down one of the pretty tree-lined residential streets when he asked, "Have you ever heard about Sienna? Skye's biological mother?"

"A little bit. Not much to be honest. I know she used to be engaged to Jacob," she said carefully. She'd heard that there'd been quite a bit of drama. That Jacob had been engaged to her and she'd left him for Brian. That along with a messy paternity situation had been entirely too *Days of our Lives* for her.

Brian let out a bitter laugh. "Yeah. She was. But she told me it was over."

Shannon wanted to keep her mouth shut, wait for him to continue, and let him get it all out before she commented, but she couldn't stop her mouth. The words just flew out. "So you slept with your best friend's ex?"

Brian winced.

"Dammit. Sorry. I didn't mean to say that." She clamped her hand over her mouth and wished for the ground to open up and swallow her whole. Judging Brian for a past mistake wasn't fair. And she didn't have any of the details.

"It's all right. It's a question I'd be asking, too. The short answer is yes. I slept with her. There are a few things you should know for context, though."

Context? What did context have to do with anything when it came to messing around with your best friend's girl? Wasn't that against the bro code or something?

"I can see those wheels turning in your head, Shannon," he said, sounding resigned.

"Are they that loud?" She was grateful when her tone sounded sympathetic rather than like Judgey McJudgey Pants. No one needed that energy.

"Very," he said. "Anyway, as I was saying… I'd been half in love with Sienna for years. But for obvious reasons, I never acted on my feelings."

"That's rough, having feelings for someone who is unlikely to be able to reciprocate."

"Yeah. It was. I kept trying to date other people, but I never felt even half as much with them as I did Sienna."

Gods. Was he still in love with her? Is that why he hadn't been able to sleep with her that night? And if so, what had changed?

Brian continued as if he hadn't sent her into a tailspin of what-ifs. "Then she showed up on my front step, declaring that the engagement with Jacob was off and saying she needed somewhere to stay until she found a new place. Obviously, I let her in. It was late, so I set her up in a guest room and decided I'd call Jacob in the morning to let him know she was with me."

"Did you call him?" Shannon asked, somehow already knowing the answer.

"No. Like I said, it was late. Sienna was a mess. I led her into the kitchen so she could tell me what happened. We ended up drinking a fair amount of tequila, and then we went to bed... in separate bedrooms. Even though I had feelings for her, I wasn't interested in taking advantage of someone who was an emotional mess. Not to mention I didn't want to hurt Jacob.

"It sounds like you were trying to do the right thing," Shannon said, trying to be supportive.

"Obviously I didn't try hard enough," he said with a scoff.

Shannon paused when they ended up in front of her house. "I take that to mean you found a way to crawl into her bed anyway?"

"I didn't crawl into hers. She crawled into mine," he said bitterly. "By the time I was fully alert enough to understand what was going on, we were already way past the point of no return if you know what I mean."

"She... took advantage of you." Shannon said it so quietly he barely heard her.

"I guess that's true to a certain extent, but it wasn't as if I was unhappy when I realized I was sleeping with the woman I'd been crushing on for years." His bitterness had only intensified, and Shannon contemplated telling him he could stop. That she'd heard enough. But before she could get the words out, he started talking again. "The next morning, I couldn't stomach the idea of calling Jacob to tell him I'd taken up right where he'd left off. So I just didn't."

"I can understand that," Shannon said, placing a hand over his heart. "You didn't intentionally try to hurt anyone."

"Maybe not, but I found out later that they weren't even broken up yet. Sienna had lied to me. And not only that, but she told me she was pregnant with my child."

"Skye," Shannon added, as if either of them needed a reminder of the child in question.

"Yep. Sienna said she was mine, and I had no reason to not believe her. Not then anyway. The truth that Jacob was her biological dad came out much later." His shoulders tightened as his voice broke on the word *later*.

"I don't know what to say, Brian, other than that's a really effed-up situation," Shannon said, having no idea how to lend rock-solid support for this one.

"You don't need to say anything, really. It's in the past, and I'm over Sienna. I have my best friend back, and now there's Skye." His lips turned up into a sweet smile as he said the little girl's name. "I'm not her dad, but I am her godfather. Jacob and Yvette are happy to let me take her off their hands periodically, so it's not like I lost her from my life."

"But...?" Shannon prompted. He'd started this story as preamble for why he'd run out of her bedroom. There had to be more.

He let out a humorless laugh. "But... for months I took care of Sienna. She had a mental health crisis and needed someone. I was her only real emotional support, and that was fine right up until she dropped the bomb that Jacob was the baby's father, not me. I lost almost everything twice because of her."

"Your friendship with Jacob and your daughter," Shannon said, trying to ignore the ache in her chest.

"And Sienna. I did love her. In my own way," he said, this time not looking at Shannon.

"All right, but what does that have to do with me?" Shannon finally prompted.

He didn't hesitate to look her in the eye. "I haven't slept with anyone since that disastrous night, Shannon. It's not that I don't want to. I do. Very much. But I guess I'm also partly terrified that if I get involved with someone I really care about it's going to blow up in my face again."

As Brian's gaze bored into Shannon's, she couldn't shake the full-body shudder that overtook her. The gorgeous man in front of her just told her, in his own way, that he'd freaked when she'd invited him to bed because he was afraid of losing her.

"I'm not interested in a hot fling or a one-night stand," he said. "I want something that lasts, and I guess, in my mind, sex before an emotional connection is the kiss of death."

Had he really just said that he didn't want a one-and-done relationship? That he cared enough to pass up sex? That meant he wanted more from a relationship. And she was just the girl who could give it to him.

"I don't want to mess this up with you, Shannon," he said. "I like you far too much."

Shannon felt her cheeks flush again and dipped her head, trying to hide it.

He laughed. "You're damned cute when you're laughing and turning all shades of purple."

"Ha, ha. Funny." Only it wasn't funny at all. Brian had just confirmed that, given half a chance, he wanted a relationship. But did she? Staring at him with a fresh perspective, she took in his long limbs and muscular arms and decided there was far more to him than she'd ever realized. She hadn't given him nearly enough credit. The fact was, she knew exactly what she'd been craving all along.

Family, connections, commitment. She wanted it all and had known it for a while. Was there a possibility Brian wanted that, too? Maybe, but did he want it enough to overcome his fear of commitment and/or abandonment? She was suddenly more than willing to find out.

"Come here," she said softly.

Brian didn't hesitate. His arms went around her, and the two of them hugged as if there were no tomorrow. Then he brushed his lips over her jaw. All it took was a turn of her head, and their lips met again. The kiss was passionate, desperate, full of emotion. And although she'd already declared that he shouldn't come inside, Shannon couldn't just walk away and wait an entire week to see him again.

"Will you come here for dinner tomorrow? I have the afternoon off. I'm not the most fabulous cook, but I do a few things well."

"I wouldn't miss it for the world," he said quickly, all the weariness draining right off him and into the atmosphere.

"Just don't break my heart," Shannon said. Then she turned around and disappeared into the house.

CHAPTER 11

"So. Looks like you've decided to stop torturing the poor bastard," Silas said from his spot on the couch in the living room.

Shannon tossed her keys into the bowl next to the front door and smirked at her brother. "Nosy much?"

"It's not nosy when you're making out right next to the window. It's not like I could miss all the spit-swapping and butt-groping."

"No one was groping anyone's butt." Not that she hadn't wanted to. Goodness that man was hot.

Silas snickered. "Please. You were five seconds from mauling him."

"That's..." She shook her head. "We are not talking about this."

A bark of laughter followed her as she made her way into the kitchen to make a half pot of decaf coffee.

Silas appeared and pulled a cheesecake out of the refrigerator. Without even asking, he served up two slices.

Shannon glanced over and smiled to herself. He knew her

so well. She took his cue and poured two cups of coffee then joined him at the table.

"Thanks, Sis."

"Right back at ya."

They took a moment to savor their dessert, but after a few bites, Shannon couldn't wait any longer. "What did Lorna say?"

The small smile he'd been wearing since she'd arrived home quickly vanished. "It's not worth it. She says six months. The media storm and the hell Mom will cause between now and my birthday are too big a cost."

Shannon was afraid of that. "You know she can't force you to do anything you don't want to do, right?"

"She can if she blackmails me," he said glumly.

"So, let's work through the worst-case scenarios. She torpedoes any new offers that come in over the next eight months. You still have your show. The minute you turn eighteen, you can fire her and go with someone you trust."

"Someone like you?" he asked hopefully.

"Don't start with that," she said with a laugh. He'd been telling her for years he wished she was his manager instead of their mother. While she understood where he was coming from, Shannon was far from the ideal candidate. She didn't have the connections needed for that type of work. "I'd be terrible for your career."

He sat up straighter and stared her dead in the eye. "No. You wouldn't. Listen, Shan, I'm not sure you understand what has happened since *Timekeeper Academy* has taken off. Offers roll in on their own. And if I want something, all Mom has to do is make a phone call. That leads to either a private audition or a meeting with the casting director or even sometimes the producers. It's not like it was before. Doors are wide open. What I need is someone who understands me and will advocate for what I want, not the biggest paycheck or how to turn me into some global tabloid name that has nothing to do with the acting I want to do."

Shannon blinked at him, feeling blindsided by the fact that she hadn't realized his reality had changed that much. When was the last time they'd talked? Really talked? "Wow, Si. That's an incredible place to be. Congratulations."

He closed his eyes and sighed. "It would be if I had any say in how my career is being handled. Mom is only interested in the biggest paychecks and the most buzz. I just want to do good work."

She reached across the table and covered his hand with hers. "I understand. If there was something I could do, you know I would."

He let out a small chuckle. "Anything except be my manager."

"What am I supposed to do? Leave my life here? You know how much I love it. I'd lose my mind in LA."

He pursed his lips and narrowed one eye, giving her an appraising look. "Hey, Shan?"

"Yeah?"

"Welcome to the twenty-first century. You know all that technology they invented? That means facetime calls, video chats, instant access. You wouldn't need to live in LA to manage my career."

Shannon scoffed. "Right. What about all those business meetings, lunches, and schmoozing Mom participates in? Are you telling me none of that is necessary?"

"Nope. That's her trying to cozy up to everyone in the business. She wants connections so she can push her other clients. And that's fine. But I don't need that. Not now anyway." He tilted his head to the side and stared right at her.

"You can do the job from here, Shannon. Please tell me you'll at least think about it. I am going to find someone else once my birthday rolls around. I'd rather it be you than anyone else. You understand the industry. But more importantly, you understand and care about me."

A ton of emotion hit Shannon all at once. Her desire to wrap him in a bubble to protect him was the strongest. But second was pure love for the kid. He deserved so much better than what their mom had to give. How could she say no to him? Silas was the most important person in her life. She knew deep down that if he begged her to move to LA she'd probably do it. She'd hate it. But she'd do it. "We have eight months, right?"

"Yeah." He nodded, but his expression was guarded.

"I'll think about it. If I decide to take this on, I'll set up an office here and do it on a trial basis. If not, I'll help you find new management, someone you can trust."

He beamed at her. "Thanks, Shannon. You have no idea how much I appreciate this."

She did know. Hadn't she been in his same shoes a decade earlier? Well, not quite the same shoes. She hadn't been on a hit television show. But she'd had some minor success, and if she'd had someone in her corner who cared more about her wellbeing than the payout, she might've stuck it out longer. Or not. It was hard to say. Acting had been fun, but she couldn't say she missed it at all. If it had been her passion, wouldn't she have cared more when she walked away? Probably.

"Come on, kid. Let's watch a movie and relax." She got up from the table, placed their dishes into the sink, and followed him into the living room where they flopped down on the couch. Shannon grabbed the remote and said, "Now, you can tell me all about Levi."

"There's nothing to tell," he said, but he couldn't hide the smile that claimed his lips.

"Right. When are you seeing him again?" She turned the television on and started scrolling through movies to stream.

"Tomorrow. But before you get all gooey-eyed and start assuming anything, we're just friends going on a hike."

She glanced over at him. "Anyone else going? Candy? Or what about their friend Axel?"

"Who's Axel?"

"Candy and Levi's friend. Pretty sure he plays for your team."

Silas's smile vanished, and he started scrolling through his phone until he landed on Levi's name. Then he started to type out a message.

Shannon laughed and gently patted his knee. "Oh, honey. You just keep sticking to that 'just friends' thing. We'll see how that turns out."

"Shut up," he said, rolling his eyes. "I'm just asking if he wants to invite anyone else."

"Really?" Shannon raised her eyebrows curiously. "Why?"

He cut her a side-eye glance. "Because I'm not a jerk?"

"Because you want to check out the competition? Or you want to evaluate all your options?"

"That's very shallow of you, Shan. Maybe I just want to make friends," he countered.

"Right," she muttered. "Just like I want to be friends with the blonde Brian brought to Yvette's wedding."

This time Silas laughed. "Okay. I might be a little curious." But when the return text came in, Silas's smile turned sweet and he slid down in the couch, settling in to keep texting.

"What did he say?" Shannon prompted.

"It's going to be just us. He said he hadn't even thought to invite them and he's pretty sure they both have to work anyway."

"Well then. Sounds like we both have dates tomorrow."

His grin widened as he went back to texting his new friend. Shannon turned to the television and picked the latest rom-com, knowing Silas was lost in his phone for the foreseeable future.

SHANNON WORKED at A Spoonful of Magic in the morning and then spent the rest of her day puttering around her house. Silas was off hiking with Levi, and Brian wouldn't be over until the evening.

By midafternoon after practically cleaning her place from top to bottom, she was starting to get anxious about her date. She'd had a moment of weakness when she invited him over. It was those kisses. They were enough to rattle anyone's brain. She hadn't been prepared to invite him in the night before. Not when she needed to talk to Silas about his meeting with Lorna. At the same time, she couldn't wait until Friday to see him either.

Hell. She was probably making a mistake. But even if that was the case, she knew she wouldn't regret giving him a shot. There was just something about Brian Knox that flipped all her switches.

It was just dinner? Right?

Sure. She chuckled to herself and strode off to the kitchen to bake her favorite chocolate caramel torte. Because even though she already knew he was completely into her, she still wanted to impress him. And better yet, this wasn't something she could pull off with just a wave of her wand.

She needed to use her own two hands. She just hoped he appreciated it.

A few hours later, with the perfect torte in the refrigerator and dinner warming in the oven, Shannon fixed her lipstick one last time and sat down with a glass of wine to wait. She'd only gotten through half her glass when she heard a commotion in front of her house. Loud voices were shouting and calling for someone.

Shannon rushed to the front door and tore it open, finding Silas and Levi in the middle of her yard. Silas's arms were around the other young man as he whispered something into his ear.

A group of about five photographers surrounded the two teenagers, each of them shooting out questions as they snapped picture after picture.

"Silas! Is this your boyfriend?"

"Did you come up to Keating Hollow for a romantic getaway?"

"Why weren't you at the press conference yesterday for your new show?"

"Can I get an interview? Your boyfriend is welcome."

"Does this mean you're officially out now? Are you gay or bi? Or do you not label yourself?"

Holy hell! How had the paparazzi found him? And why was he hugging Levi like that in front of them? Silas never shared his personal life with the press. To be open about his sexuality now was a strange choice, especially since, as far as Shannon knew, the two weren't actually dating.

She hurried through the circle of photographers to Silas's side. "What are you doing? You know this is going to cause a media shitstorm," she whispered into his ear. Then without waiting for his answer, she spoke louder, so everyone could hear her. "Let's get you both inside. I think you paps have enough to work with, don't you?"

Silas flashed her an irritated look and whispered in her ear, "Levi twisted his ankle. I was trying to help him inside when the photographers showed up. Right after they rushed toward us, he stumbled over a sprinkler head and I caught him. That's it."

Crap. That explained a lot. "Has he seen a healer?"

"Yes," Silas said through gritted teeth. "But Hope and Chad are over at the coast today. I didn't want him to be alone, so I brought him back here. Big mistake." He turned his attention back to Levi. "Sorry, man. I know this sucks."

"Can we just go inside?" he asked, ignoring the photographers. "My foot is throbbing."

"Yes," Shannon said, wrapping one arm around his waist while Silas did the same. He draped one arm over each of their shoulders, and together they started to move slowly toward the front door.

"Hey. Need some help?" Brian asked, rushing to their side.

Shannon glanced up at the handsome man holding a bouquet of red roses. Damn, was that sweet or what? "We just need to get Levi inside. He sprained his ankle."

The photographers started to move in again, taking picture after picture of the four of them. Shannon dreaded what kind of story they'd come up with. Anything to sell the tabloids, she was certain.

Levi winced and one knee buckled. "Dammit," he said, his face pinched in pain.

"Didn't the healer give him a pain potion?" Shannon asked Silas.

"She tried, but he wouldn't take it. He said he didn't like the potions and that he'd take something over the counter."

"I've got this," Brian said, standing in front of Levi. "Come on, man. I'm going to lift you up and carry you inside."

Levi jerked his head up, a panicked expression in his eyes as they darted around taking in the paparazzi. "You can't do that. They'll get a photo of it."

"It's either that or video of you barely walking," Brian said. "If you just let me pick you up in a fireman's carry, we can be inside in seconds with the door closed and you on the couch. What do you say?"

His eyes darted around at the chaotic scene again, and then he closed them and nodded once. "Just get me inside."

Brian didn't hesitate. He picked up the teen, draped him over one shoulder, and strode into the house, Silas and Shannon right behind him.

Shannon slammed the door shut and quickly lowered the window shades. She rapidly skirted the downstairs, closing the rest of the blinds to make sure no more photos were taken of them. After grabbing some ibuprofen from the cabinet and a glass of water, she made her way back to the living room where Levi was sprawled on the couch. Silas was slumped in a chair, both hands covering his face, and Brian was inspecting Levi's ankle. She placed the pills and water glass on the coffee table and asked Levi, "How is it?"

"Hurts."

She nodded, shook out a few pills, and handed them over along with the water glass. "Hopefully that will help a little. What did the healer tell you to do?"

"To stay off it for a few weeks." Levi grimaced as he tried to shift his body into a more comfortable position. "It hurts like a mofo right now."

"I'm sure it—" Shannon started.

"It's not broken," Silas said, cutting her off. "That's

something at least, right? Levi said it wasn't, but the healer confirmed it. She said it's just a bad sprain and with some physio he'll be good to go by the time school starts this fall."

"Didn't she give him any crutches?" Shannon asked.

"She was out. Said she'd make sure and have a set tomorrow," Silas said. "I'll get them for him in the morning."

"You don't have to do that," Levi said with a groan. "I'm sure Hope or Chad will take care of it."

Silas slid off the chair and went to sit on the coffee table across from Levi.

Shannon retreated, grabbing Brian's hand to pull him with her. Silas clearly needed to get a few things off his chest. That wouldn't be easy with her and Brian hovering. They moved to the entry way between the kitchen and the living room. While she wanted to give them some space, she also wanted to be on hand if Levi needed anything else.

"I'm not doing anything while I'm here in Keating Hollow," Silas said. "Remember? I'm on vacation with nothing better to do… now that I've broken you. It's not a problem to grab your crutches. Besides, it's completely my fault that you got hurt."

"It wasn't your fault," Levi said, sounding slightly exasperated as if they'd already had that conversation. "I was the one not paying attention while we were climbing back down those rocks."

"But I coerced you into going up there. You didn't want to go, remember?"

He tenderly brushed a lock of hair out of Levi's eye but then quickly pulled his hand back and averted his eyes as if he was embarrassed. "Sorry."

"It's all right," Levi said softly. The two boys kept their heads together as they quietly talked about the hike and the views they'd seen before his accident.

"Come in here," Shannon said, finally giving her full attention to Brian and tugging him into the kitchen. "What happened to those flowers you were carrying earlier when you got sucked into the middle of that Hollywood garbage."

He frowned. "Um, I think I handed them over to Silas before I carried Levi in the house."

She glanced around, found nothing, and then retreated back to the living room. She didn't see them anywhere, so she barked out, "Who took my roses?"

Silas pointed at the chair he'd been sitting in before he'd launched himself at Levi. "In the storage pocket. Sorry, was distracted I guess."

"Uh-huh," Shannon agreed, but didn't put any feeling behind her words. Instead she rescued her flowers from the pocket on the side of the chair and took them back into the kitchen. She turned and smiled at Brian. "These are beautiful. Thank you."

He stepped in close and wrapped one arm around her. "Not as beautiful as you."

Her heart melted. It was completely gone. She laid the flowers on the counter, reached up with both hands, cupping his cheeks, and pressed her lips to his.

Brian let out a soft murmur of approval, pulling her in even closer. "I've been thinking about this all day."

"Me, too," she admitted and kissed him again, this time opening to—

The doorbell rang, followed by loud knocking.

"Seriously?" Shannon pulled back and stalked into the living room, already pulling her phone out of her pocket. It was one thing to stand on public property and take pictures of her house, it was entirely another to harass them.

"This is Drew Baker," the deputy sheriff said into the phone.

"Hey. It's Shannon Ansell. We've got a paparazzi problem over here at my house. Do you think you can—"

"Shannon!" a woman called from the other side of the door. "Open up. I don't have my key."

"Mom?" Shannon rushed to the door and looked through the peephole. Dread coiled in her gut. What the hell was she doing there?

"Shannon?" Deputy Sheriff Baker asked on the phone. "Everything all right? I can be there in five minutes."

"Hold on. I think I might've been mistaken." With the phone still to her ear, she pulled the door open to find the paparazzi was gone and the only person who remained was Gigi Ansell.

CHAPTER 12

"Sorry, Drew. I was mistaken. Everything is fine here," Shannon said into the phone as she stared at her mother. The woman was dressed in a flawless white silk jumpsuit, red six-inch heels, and had a red silk scarf around her neck despite the fact it was over eighty degrees.

"No problem. Call me if you need anything," Drew said.

Shannon mumbled her thanks and ended the call.

"Well? Aren't you going to let me into my own house?" Gigi said.

"Of course," Shannon said, snapping out of her frozen state. She pulled the door open wider and made room for her mom to enter the small cottage.

Gigi waved toward the driveway. "Someone needs to get my luggage from the car."

Silas stood, his fists clenched and his jaw tight as he glared at her. "You couldn't even give me a few days? Dammit, Gigi. I needed a break from everything Hollywood."

Both Shannon and her mother knew he meant he needed a break from Gigi. Their mother rolled her eyes and then looked down at Levi, who was now sitting upright, his injured ankle propped up on pillows.

"Who is this?" Gigi asked, peering over her glasses at him, her nose wrinkled as if something smelled foul.

"This is Levi. He's—" Shannon started to tell her he was her friend's brother so that Silas wouldn't have to explain anything to her.

But Silas cut her off and said, "He does Shannon's yard work."

Both Levi and Shannon stared at him, their mouths slightly open.

"Oh." Gigi frowned. "What's he doing on my couch?"

Shannon bristled at the way she was claiming ownership of the house and all the things in it. It was true, her parents owned the place. It had been her grandmother's, and they'd never sold it after she passed. But all the stuff in it? It had either been left by her grandmother or Shannon had bought it herself.

"He sprained his ankle," Silas said tightly. "He's resting here until his sister gets home and can care for him."

Levi carefully lifted his injured foot off the pillows, and with a guarded expression, he said, "That's not really necessary. I'll be fine on my own couch. I should get out of here and let Mrs. Ansell have her house back."

It's not her house, Shannon's inner voice wanted to scream.

"What?" Silas sat back down on the coffee table, facing him. "No. You can't walk. What if you need something to eat or drink? Or can't find the remote?"

Levi glared at him. "I'll be fine." He glanced past Silas. "Brian? Do you think you could help me get home?"

"Sure, man. No problem." Without missing a beat, Brian moved toward the front door. Just as he opened it, he said,

"Let me move the SUV into the driveway then I'll help you out."

"But what about your date?" Silas asked then grimaced when he met Shannon's stormy gaze. "Never mind."

"What date? Who is this man?" Gigi asked, eyeing him suspiciously.

Shannon threw her hands up. "He's my date, Mother. But we can reschedule."

Brian glanced back at her, giving her a reassuring smile, and then disappeared outside.

"That man is your date?" Gigi asked Shannon, her expression calculating. "Is he the reason you won't come home to Los Angeles?"

"Los Angeles isn't my home," Shannon said, knowing it wouldn't do any good. Her mother only heard what she wanted to hear.

Gigi waved a dismissive hand, barely sparing Levi a glance as she gracefully lowered herself into the overstuffed chair. "Aren't you going to offer me a drink?"

Shannon lost it. "It's your house, remember? Besides, someone needs to get your luggage. I guess that'd be me, right? Silas shouldn't go outside. Not after the circus that was just here. They could still be out there waiting. So if you want a drink, the kitchen is that way." She pointed to the back of the house. "Just in case you forgot where it was."

Gigi's eyes narrowed, and she gave her daughter a disapproving frown. "Shannon, there is no reason to be rude."

I could say the same to you. The words were on the tip of her tongue, but she swallowed them. Fighting wasn't going to do anything but give her a migraine. "Where is the key to your rental?"

Gigi held a key fob out to her daughter even as she turned

her attention to Silas. "I hope you enjoyed your little weekend escape. But you know it's time to get back to work."

Silas glared at her in icy silence.

She sighed. "Don't pull that television-star-diva crap on me, Si. We both know how that's going to end."

Levi cleared his throat.

Silas and Gigi both turned to look at him.

"Do you need something?" Silas asked, the icy mask suddenly replaced with concern as he rested one hand on Levi's forearm.

Levi glanced down at Silas's hand before gently removing it. "I just need help getting outside. Then you two can have your conversation in private."

Silas's shoulders hunched, and Shannon knew he'd felt that silent rejection deeply. Despite his flirty, extrovert persona, he'd always been sensitive. He probably knew he'd messed up when he called Levi the lawn guy. But Shannon knew exactly why he'd done that. He hadn't wanted Gigi to get the idea that Levi was someone he cared about. Or even someone that he had potential to care about. It was safer for Levi if he wasn't on Gigi's radar at all. He'd be either dismissed or used in whatever plan she had to control Silas. But Levi couldn't know that. Not after only knowing Silas for a couple of days.

Brian strode back in. "Okay, ready, Levi?"

Levi nodded.

Silas held out a hand. Levi hesitated for a moment but then took it and the one Brian held out for him before hauling himself up while standing on his good leg. The pair of them let him lean on them as he hobbled out on one leg.

Gigi turned to Shannon. "What's going on there?"

"Levi and Silas are just friends, Mom. They went hiking

today, and Levi sprained an ankle. There's really nothing to talk about."

"They went hiking?" Her voice rose a few octaves, and she sat up straight in the chair, color rising on her angular cheeks. "Silas risked his physical health by going hiking? I told you how detrimental it would be to his reality show if he were to end up flat on his back for a few weeks. The activities we already have planned would be out of the question!"

Shannon ignored her rant and went back into the kitchen. The dinner she'd made was still warming in the oven. So much for a romantic dinner for two. The pesto salmon wouldn't taste nearly as good if she had to share it with her mother. Shannon's stomach lurched with the idea of eating anything.

Frustrated, she turned the oven off, pulled the pan out of the oven, and then grabbed a glass and the nearest bottle of wine. After taking a swig right out of the bottle, she poured some into the glass and took it to her mother, who'd followed the boys outside and was standing on the porch, staring at Brian's SUV. Or rather, she was staring at Silas, who was standing next to the passenger door and talking to Levi through the open window.

Nosy much? Shannon contemplated downing the glass of wine, but instead pressed it into her mother's hand and took off for the rented Mercedes sitting next to the SUV in her driveway.

"Let me do that for you," Brian said, meeting her at the trunk of the rental car.

She glanced over at him. "You don't have to do that. It's nice of you to take Levi home. I'm sure the last place he wants to be is here with Bellatrix."

Brian chuckled. "No worries. Levi and Silas are working

some things out, so I have a few minutes to spare." He gave her a small smile. "I'm sorry our date was interrupted."

"I'm the one who's sorry," Shannon said. "I had no idea she would show up tonight. She threatened to come up here, but since she hasn't been here in over a decade, I thought it was mostly bluster. Besides, Silas's deadline to fall into step was tomorrow. I figured we'd get at least one more threatening phone call before she pounced." She tugged an oversized suitcase out of the trunk. She grunted when she realized the thing weighed more than she did.

"I've got this one. You get the two smaller ones," Brian said.

Shannon retrieved the rest of the luggage, and together they hauled it inside.

"Where do you want this?" Brian asked.

Shannon cringed. Where was she going to put her mother? She really had no choice, did she? "Upstairs. The room on the right."

She followed him to the second floor to the master bedroom. The cottage was only a two-bedroom house. The only place to put her mother was in her room. Silas already had the spare. That left Shannon on the couch.

"This is your room, isn't it?" Brian asked.

Shannon nodded and stared at the bed. Her cheeks flushed with heat as she remembered changing the sheets that morning just in case the date turned into more than dinner. At least she didn't need to do anything to prepare for her mother to sleep there. Well... she might need to remove a few things from her nightstand. If her mother found them, she'd die of embarrassment.

Brian gave her his trademark mischievous grin. "My door is open if you need another place to sleep. I have a really comfortable bed."

"That's a little presumptuous, don't you think?" she asked, returning his grin even as she shook her head.

"What? I was talking about my guest room. But if you prefer to cuddle, I can make room for you in my king-size bed." He stepped in close and ran his thumb over her cheek. "In fact, I think that sounds like the best idea I've had all day."

"Tell me something, Brian," Shannon whispered.

"Anything."

She tilted her head to the side and studied him. "How many times have you thought about getting me into your bed today?"

"Probably about twice as many times as you thought of getting me into yours," he said with a laugh.

"So... that's what you spent most of the day thinking about then?" she teased.

"You got it." He brushed a soft kiss over her lips. "Call me when you get a chance or if you just need to vent. Once your mother is out of your hair, we'll reschedule. And let me know if Friday is still on."

"Friday is still on," she said. "Even if she's still here bothering us, I'm going. It's the bet, right?"

"I was going to let you bend the rules a little considering the extenuating circumstances."

Shannon shook her head. She wasn't going to let her mother ruin this too. "Nope. Rules are rules. Where are you taking me?"

"A Touch of Magic," he said, his eyes twinkling. "Special couple's massage. You up for it?"

She swallowed hard, imagining him naked under the massage table's sheet. "You're serious?"

"Yep." His eyes glinted as he continued. "They started something new for date night packages. Catered romantic dinners on the patio, massages and one other service of the couple's choice."

She laughed. "You mean like pedicures or facials?"

"Sure. Or body scrubs, wraps, meditation. I'll let it be your choice."

Most of the tension that had arrived with her mother vanished as she imagined relaxing at the spa later that week with Brian by her side. "You're something else. You know that, right?"

"Something annoying? Ridiculous? Extra?" he asked, barely holding back his own laughter.

"Something special," she whispered and rose up on her tiptoes to kiss him again.

CHAPTER 13

*B*rian sat at his breakfast counter, nursing a cup of coffee. His head was killing him, and he silently berated himself for having one too many glasses of wine the night before. After he'd gotten Levi home and set up on his couch with everything he'd need from water to snacks, Brian had gone home, and instead of eating dinner, he drank it.

The scene at Shannon's house had been something out of a bad romantic comedy. The paparazzi mess was one tier of crazy, but Shannon's mother was a whole other level of insanity. The woman was everything about his life he'd been happy to leave behind in southern California. She was selfish, rude, pretentious, and was obviously tearing Silas up. Shannon hadn't been thrilled to see her, but Brian could see that Shannon had years of training in handling the woman. She'd be all right. Brian just wished there was something he could do to make the situation better for both of them.

His smartphone went off right at the same time as his office line. He groaned, pressing a palm to his forehead. When was the painkiller he took going to kick in?

He glanced at his smartphone and promptly ignored it when he saw Cara's name flashing on the screen. And he seriously considered letting the business line go to voicemail, but he didn't like doing that. If there was one thing he was good at, it was running his business and staying accessible to his business partners.

"Brian Knox," he said into the phone while rubbing one temple.

"Brian!" his father barked. "What in the hell do you not understand about laying low until this deal is done?"

Brian pulled the phone away from his ear and stared at it as if it could tell him why his father was so pissed. When he heard his father ranting again, he put the phone up to his ear and said, "I have no idea what you're talking about."

"Have you not gone online yet this morning? It's everywhere," his father said. "Open GNT. That will give you the worst of it."

"GNT? The gossip blog?" Brian asked. The site's official name was *Gossip n Tea,* and it seemed to break all the juiciest celebrity news first these days. "Why would I want to go there?"

"Because you're in the headline. Seems the ex-southern California playboy has found love with Silas Ansell's big sister." He'd taken on a mocking tone, indicating that his father was reading straight from the headline.

Brian's stomach rolled with unease as he pulled the webpage up. Sure enough, the headline indicated that he and Shannon were an item, and below it they'd inserted a picture of the two of them holding hands outside of her house with Silas at the SUV, talking with Levi. It had been taken when Shannon walked him back out to his SUV after bringing in her mother's luggage. "Son of a..." He let out a growl. "I thought the paparazzi had already left."

"You know better than that, son," his father said, sounding annoyed. "That's not all. There's big news of Silas Ansell suing for emancipation, so this story isn't going to go away any time soon. I'm assuming his sister is the woman you told me about? The one you're bringing to Brittany's wedding?"

"Yes." How had news gotten out about Silas? Lorna would never betray a client's trust. Not to mention that, according to Shannon, Silas had decided against suing his parents and instead was just going to wait it out until his birthday. "It's not true, Dad. Silas isn't suing his parents."

"Doesn't matter. You know how the rumor mill works. As long as there is something to talk about, they'll report it even if facts don't line up. I need you to get down here today. Manchester has lost his mind over there, and we have a mess to clean up."

A strong sense of déjà vu washed over him. Hadn't they already had this conversation? "We already talked about this. I don't care what Manchester says or does. I'm not going anywhere. I have commitments here." It was the complete truth. He was giving a drum lesson to Levi later that day, unless the teenager decided to stay home and rest his ankle. He'd have to wait and see.

"You're about to care. The man is threatening to file a fraud suit against both of us if we can't get him to back down," his father said.

"Fraud? What? Why?" Brian was so perplexed he couldn't even seem to form coherent thoughts.

"It's a totally bogus lawsuit, but the man has more money than Warren Buffet. If he wants to waste some of it to make our lives hell, that's what he's going to do. The Knox

Corporation can withstand the blow if it comes to that. Can yours?"

The answer was unequivocally *no*. His company could not withstand a drawn-out lawsuit, no matter how frivolous. He just didn't have the kind of reserves that the Knox Corporation did. Brian was mostly a one-man show with a few customer service reps who were individual contractors. "So what do you propose? You want me to come down there and beg him not to sue me? That's not going to work."

"You need to get down here and work something out with Cara so she'll call him off. That's what you need to do. And you need to stop ignoring her calls. I'm setting up a meeting for tomorrow morning. Get on the next available flight. Your mother and I will be expecting you."

Brian let out a sigh of defeat. "Fine. I'll text you my flight information."

"Good. And Brian?"

"Yeah, Dad?"

His father cleared his throat. "Have you ever had a relationship with Cara? Physical or otherwise?"

"No."

"I see." His father paused before adding, "You don't deserve this, and I'm sorry I ever bought into the idea that you and Cara would be a good match. It seemed like a good idea at the time. We'll work it out. See you tonight."

Stunned, Brian didn't say anything at first. Then he mimicked his father, clearing his own throat, and said, "Thanks."

After Brian ended the call with his father, he picked up his smartphone and frowned when he saw that Cara had called three times and left numerous texts. They were all a version of her begging him to call her. She said it was important and she couldn't believe he'd done this to her. The entire thing was crazy, and he wanted to throw his phone against the wall. But that wouldn't solve anything. Instead, he took a deep breath and called her back.

"Brian!" Cara practically screamed into the phone. "What are you trying to do to me?"

"I'm not doing anything to you, Cara. Why is your father threatening to sue me and my father? You don't honestly think that's the best way to get my attention, do you?" He was spitting mad, and he knew chewing her out probably wasn't a good idea. But dammit, his dad was right; he didn't deserve this.

"You're making me look like a fool," she whispered into the phone, sounding as if she was moments away from crying.

"How? I don't understand. So our families made a few mentions about us becoming a power couple. That has never translated into us *being* a couple. One date to a wedding doesn't suddenly morph into a relationship."

"I know that," she said, sniffling. "I'm sorry. It's just that I was asked to be interviewed for *Cali Style* recently, and the article came out today. I might have talked about you a little. Now I look like the biggest fool in Los Angeles. You could have warned a girl."

"You mentioned me in an article?" he asked, confused. "Why?"

"Well, I was going up there for the wedding and I thought… You know what I thought. I might have alluded to things I now know you were never interested in. I mean, it's always been a given that we'd give it a go at some point, right? You offered to let me stay with you for goodness sake. What was I supposed to think?"

"That a friend was offering you a place to stay so that you

didn't have to drive an hour to get to the nearest available hotel?" Brian felt like he'd entered an alternate reality. She couldn't be serious, could she? He'd known she was a little spoiled and self-centered, but she'd also been sweet and kind. As far as he'd been concerned, she was harmless. Man, he'd called that one wrong, hadn't he?

"That's just… Well, that's not what happened, and now I'm going to be the laughing stock of my social circle. You're just going to have to help me make this right." She sounded resentful and defensive now. The fact that he hadn't backed down from his indignation was likely the reason that she was pushing back. More arguing on the phone wasn't going to get him what he wanted. "Fine. I'll be there tonight. We can talk tomorrow after I meet with your father."

"You will?" her tone was hopeful now, as if he'd asked her on a date instead of confirming that they'd figure this mess out.

"Yes. And by the time I leave, we'll have put this behind us, with you going your way and me going mine. No more talk of marriage or dating. It's just not going to happen."

"Because of Shannon Ansell," she said bitterly.

"No, Cara, because I'm happy living in northern California in a tiny magical village, and you will always be part of the social fabric of southern California. We just don't fit," he said.

"But we could. I like Keating Hollow," she said.

It was a lie. She might like it for a short retreat or a romantic vacation, but Cara Manchester would hate living in the redwoods. Her beloved social circle was in Los Angeles. Not that any of that mattered. He just wasn't interested. "I'll see you tomorrow," he said again. "So we can untangle this mess with your father."

"Okay. Text me when your plane lands. Bye!" She ended the

call, and Brian sank into his office chair, holding his head in his hands. How had he gotten mixed up in this mess?

Right. Brian Knox was supposed to run his father's company one day, and that meant marrying the right girl. But when he defected from the company, he thought he'd left all of that behind. He was just finding out how wrong he was.

Reluctantly, he typed the words *Cali Style* into his browser and hit *Search*.

CHAPTER 14

"*H*ere. Can you believe we're doing this instead of spending the day at the beach like we planned?" Shannon refilled Silas's coffee mug and topped off her own. They'd been roused by their mother an hour ago and tasked with sifting through the media to evaluate the damage while she worked her contacts to spin the gossip to Silas's advantage. Or, as Silas had pointed out, more like to *her* advantage.

"Don't remind me," Silas muttered.

So far, the worst stories were the ones that used the picture of Silas holding Levi up after he tripped in the yard and then outed Silas and named Levi as his new boyfriend. They made up claims about Silas running away from LA for a torrid weekend with his boyfriend after his parents disapproved of the relationship. The worst part was that Silas and Levi were so close in the picture that it made it look like they were getting ready to kiss, which made the stories look plausible.

Silas was sick over the fact that Levi's face was all over the internet because of him. "The lies, Shannon. It's so gross how they say anything regardless of the truth. I can't imagine what he's thinking right now."

"Have you called him?" She sat down and passed him a piece of toast.

"I sent him a text asking him to call me when he wakes up." He closed his eyes and took a deep breath. "After yesterday, I doubt he'll text me back. What was I thinking, introducing him to Mom as the yard boy? Ack! How tone deaf am I?"

She gave him a sympathetic pat on his arm. "You were trying to keep him off Mom's radar. And honestly, Si, it was probably the best thing you could've done. You know what a snob she is. She never would've given him another thought if these pictures hadn't surfaced."

"It doesn't matter now. The damage is done, and he's likely never to talk to me again." Silas dropped his head to the table and let out a groan of frustration.

Shannon felt for him. There was no telling how Levi would feel about being pulled into the Hollywood drama. "What did he say yesterday when you apologized for the way you introduced him?"

"He wasn't happy. He said it made him feel like he was nothing." He blinked his eyes open. "I don't blame him, Shan. It sounded so shitty when I heard it come out of my mouth. I just didn't want her to know that I like him. You know how she is."

"Did you tell him that?"

He sat back up. "Yeah, but it might be too little too late. He has a history of being made to feel unimportant. The last thing I want to do is make him feel that way again."

Shannon bit down on her lower lip. "You might have to do more than send a text. You know, some gesture to show that you care."

"It's only been a few days. It's not like we're dating or anything. What exactly am I supposed to do?"

"You'll figure it out." Shannon clicked on yet another article, and to her surprise, this one wasn't about Silas. It was about her and Brian. "What the... Why would anyone care about what I'm doing or who I'm doing it with?"

"Huh?" Silas shifted to look over her shoulder at the picture of her and Brian holding hands as they walked to the SUV. He let out a little growl. "They can't even leave my sister alone. Crap, Shan, I'm sorry."

But Shannon shook her head. "I don't think this has anything to do with you. It says Brian is tied to some woman named Cara Manchester and that I'm the other woman. What?" She frantically Googled Cara Manchester, and the first article that came up made her cry out, "He has a fiancée!"

The headline of the lead story for *Cali Style* read: "Manchester and Knox Celebrate Two Perfect Unions."

Below the headline there were two pictures. One was a picture of Brian and the pixie he'd brought to Yvette and Jacob's wedding. They had their arms wrapped around each other's waists and were smiling as if they were the happiest two people in the world. The caption read: *Southern California's most anticipated wedding.* The other photo was of the two CEOs of the Manchester and Knox corporations.

Bile rose in the back of Shannon's throat. How could he be engaged? He swore they were just friends. She'd been there at the wedding when Shannon had danced with Brian. She and Brian had even kissed right in front of her! Maybe they had some sort of open relationship? The thought made her want to vomit.

"Maybe the article is wrong," Silas said. "You know how reporters can be."

Shannon glanced at him. "It's an interview in a reputable style magazine, not an article in a gossip rag. Has a magazine who interviewed you ever gotten it *that* wrong?"

He slowly shook his head and took the computer away from her. "I don't know what to say, Shan. I'm sorry."

Tears stung the backs of her eyes, but she blinked them back, determined not to cry. It wasn't as if she was in a relationship with Brian. They had a bet. That was it. And since he was engaged, she was calling it off. No way was she getting in the middle of that mess. She grabbed her phone, tapped out a text to Brian, and hit *Send* before she could think too hard about it.

How had she gone from living her quiet life in Keating Hollow and managing A Spoonful of Magic, to becoming the 'other woman' in the Hollywood gossip rags overnight? She'd known that Brian was from Los Angeles and came from a powerful family, but they weren't in entertainment. She'd never suspected dating him would lead her right back to the world she'd consciously decided to leave behind.

Her phone buzzed. She saw it was from Brian and shut her phone off.

"What did you text him?" Silas asked.

"I told him the bet was void, due to the fact he was engaged and didn't tell me, and that all future dates are canceled effective immediately." Her heart sped up, and her entire body heated as her anxiety kicked in. She took a deep breath, reminding herself that she hadn't done anything wrong. Brian was a jackass and deserved every ounce of her wrath. "I also might have called him a few names that aren't safe for underage ears."

Silas rolled his eyes. "I'm not eight."

"I know. I'm just... I don't want to talk about it."

"Got it." He closed his computer. "Looks like we've both got relationship problems."

Shannon nodded. "I think yours is salvageable, though. Mine is just over."

Silas raised his eyebrows. "You're not even going to let him explain?"

"What's there to talk about? Cara Manchester thinks they are engaged. That there's going to be a wedding next year. Have you ever heard of a bride thinking there was a wedding without informing the groom?"

"Stranger things have happened in Hollywood," Silas said ruefully.

"Please. I want nothing to do with that nonsense." Shannon got up out of her chair and moved into the kitchen. "Are you ready for a real breakfast? I'm fixing eggs and bacon."

Silas practically drooled. "Bacon? Do you know how long it's been since I've had any real bacon?"

"Since I made it for you last?" She grabbed her wand from the counter, gave it a wave, and stood there watching as her kitchen went to work.

"That's one heck of a gift you have there, Sis," Silas said.

"You know I could teach you how to do it, right? It's not like we don't share the same air magic gift." She eyed him. "Do you even use your magic these days?"

He shrugged. "Not often. Sometimes for work when I do stunts. Or when I'm too lazy to get up and get the remote."

She nodded in understanding. "Not into showing off down there among the stars?"

"Not really. They always want me to perform like a show pony. I get enough of that from my day job." He leaned back in his chair, pointed at the last remaining croissant on the counter and then back to himself. The pastry flew toward him, but it moved so fast it smacked him in the head and flopped onto the table in front of him.

Shannon laughed even though her insides still felt like they were crumbling after the news about Brian. "I can see why you don't show off your remarkable skills. Wouldn't want to take someone's eye out."

Silas chuckled and then tore off a piece of the croissant and shoved it into his mouth.

"Is that bacon I smell?" Gigi Ansell asked as she walked into the kitchen. "I hope it's the turkey variety. Silas can't afford a breakout right now. You know what greasy food does to his complexion."

"Sure, I can," Silas said, sounding defiant as he leaped to his feet and pressed his palms on the table. "I'm not doing that reality show. You can't force me into it, so it's best if you just call them right now and tell them it isn't happening."

"Oh, Silas," she said dismissively. "You always say stuff like this when you feel like slacking off. But then you think about your career and you do what's best for your long-term goals. We'll talk about it after breakfast. But no bacon." She turned to Shannon. "No wonder you've put on a few pounds. You know that stuff isn't good for you."

"Mom, my weight is none of your business. I might not be Hollywood skinny, thank the gods, but my healer thinks I'm right where I'm supposed to be." *So back off your bacon opinions.* Shannon knew she was scowling as she retrieved plates from the cabinet. She'd normally have let her magic deal with setting the table, but when she was angry, things usually went haywire. With the way her blood was boiling, it was likely she'd take her mother's head clear off if she tried using her wand.

"Damn, Mom. Leave Shannon alone," Silas said, moving into the kitchen to take the plates from her.

"I will, just as soon as I fix her PR mess. This Brian guy you've been dating is quite the catch," her mother said, sounding impressed.

Shannon snorted. "Right. Because dating an engaged man is the perfect way to start a relationship."

Gigi tsked and sat at the table. She wrinkled her nose at the computers and empty coffee mugs Shannon and Silas had left behind. "You might want to tidy up before we eat here, dear."

We? Shannon sighed and tossed more bacon in the pan.

"Just yogurt for me though," Gigi said. "And what does a person have to do to get a cup of coffee around here?"

"Get up and get it?" Silas said sarcastically even as he refilled both his and Shannon's mugs.

"Funny. Stop being ungrateful," she snapped and went back to scrolling through her phone.

Shannon and Silas shared an eye roll, but because neither of them was quite petty enough to actually make her get her own coffee, Shannon handed him a fresh mug and he filled it.

While Silas took the mugs to the table, Shannon plated their breakfasts, even going so far as to put her mother's yogurt in a bowl instead of leaving it in the single serving cup and adding berries the way she knew her mother liked it.

"Thank you, Shannon. That was kind of you, but I'm not eating blueberries right now," Gigi said when she looked in the bowl.

"Why?" Shannon asked, frowning. "Blueberries are a superfood. You're all about antioxidants."

Gigi gave her a patient smile. "They stain the teeth, dear. I need to be at my best when Silas and I meet with the reporters about his new show."

Silas slammed his fist down on the table so hard the utensils rattled together.

"Silas! What are you—" Gigi started.

"I. Am. Not. Doing that show. Forget it. Call them today and tell them I'm out. If you don't, I'll quit *Timekeeper*, too." His face was red, and he was visibly shaking with frustration.

Shannon rushed over to him and grabbed his hand, lending him all the support she had to give. The situation with their mother had only gotten worse. Since she'd arrived in Keating Hollow, she hadn't listened to one word Silas had said about his career. She steamrolled him at every turn, leaving him with no voice in his own life. No wonder he'd taken off and said he might not go back.

Gigi rose slowly from her chair and peered at Silas, her body as rigid as a steel pole. "You will not talk to your mother that way, young man. Do you hear me?"

"I'm not talking to my mother right now, Gigi," he spat out. "I'm talking to my manager, and what I'm saying is I will not sign that contract. I will not show up to set. And if you don't call it off, I'm not coming home just so the cameras can show up one day and start following me around. Hear me when I say I'm not doing this. If you try to force it, I'll get the lawyers involved."

"You mean like that country bumpkin lawyer, Lorna White?" she said with a sneer. "The one who leaked that you were trying to emancipate? You think she's going to protect you from the mother who made you a star? Think again, Silas. I made your career, and I can end it, too."

Silas's face turned white, and his fists were clenched so hard that Shannon wondered if his fingernails were cutting into his skin. He opened his mouth, but no sound came out. Instead he vibrated with emotion and then stalked from the room. The front door opened and slammed a second later, making the walls shake.

Shannon stared open-mouthed at her mother.

"Stop looking at me like that," Gigi said as she sat back down in her chair and took a sip of her coffee as if nothing had happened. Everything about her appeared put together. Her flowy red silk dress draped off one shoulder, making her looked casual yet sophisticated. Her dark hair was pulled up in an elegant twist, and her makeup was flawless. She even held her head high, though Shannon had no idea how she managed to do that after the horrifying scene she'd just witnessed.

But then she saw it, her mother's one tell.

Gigi Ansell put her mug down and then unconsciously cracked one of her knuckles. The moment the sound filled the silence, she stopped and pressed both hands to the table as if to stop herself from repeating the bad habit.

"I think you should go, Mom," Shannon said quietly.

To Shannon's surprise, her mother nodded and rose from her chair without an argument. But then she said, "A drive would probably help clear my head."

Shannon groaned.

"What?" Gigi demanded. "You said I should go. I'm going. I'll be back in an hour."

"I meant go back to Los Angeles." Shannon threw her hands up in the air in pure frustration. "You can't keep doing this to Silas. He's going to break, and then where will your star be?"

"He's not a delicate flower, Shannon. Mind your own business." She turned and strode into the living room.

Shannon ran to catch up with her and stood in front of the door, blocking her exit. She never thought she'd do that. "It is my business, Mom. Silas came to me for help because you're stifling him. I told him to take a few weeks off, get rested—"

"A few weeks! Do you have any idea what you're saying?" she asked, sounding horrified. "That endorsement deal won't be there in two weeks. We have to move now. After he's done sulking, revise your advice. Goodness knows he's stopped listening to me. Maybe he'll listen to you."

"There you go again, not listening to anyone," Shannon said, her voice raspy with barely controlled anger. "What I was going to say is that I think he needs a longer break than that. He needs space from you, from work, from Hollywood. It's too much, Mom. Let him stay here for the rest of summer, and when it's time for *Timekeeper* to start filming, I'll bring him back down personally and—"

"No." She reached for the doorknob, but Shannon moved in front of it, forcing her mother to either back down or physically move Shannon in order to get out the door. Gigi gritted her teeth and said, "I will not have Silas do what you did. You threw away your life when you moved back here. Silas is destined for great things. I will not let you poison his mind with your negative talk of the business. Now either help me get him back home within the next few days, or I'll make it really uncomfortable for you two to stay here."

"What do you mean when you say you'll 'make it uncomfortable' for us?" Shannon frowned at her mother. That sounded like a threat. And what would she do exactly? It was already uncomfortable enough with the paparazzi hanging around outside. Something tingled at the back of her mind with the thought of the photographers, but before she could form another thought, her mother spoke.

"Dad and I will sell this house. I will not provide a place for you two to hide out. You'll be forced to come home. There is no way you make enough at that *candy store* to buy something of your own."

Shannon didn't even bother trying to correct her mother about A Spoonful of Magic. It wasn't a candy store. They sold all kinds of confections. But that was hardly the point and not what she should be focusing on at that moment. "Sell the house?" The thought was unthinkable. She'd spent a large part of her childhood as well as all of her adult life in the small cottage. Her mother couldn't be serious, could she? "You'd throw me out of Grandma's house?"

"It's not your grandma's house anymore, Shannon. It's my house. I've allowed you to live here, rent free, mind you, for too long. It's time you got your life on track anyway. But it's your choice. Convince Silas to come home, or I'll see to it you have *no* choice."

Shannon was so stunned by Gigi's threat that when the woman reached for the doorknob again she just stepped aside and let her go. As she watched her mother walk to her rental car, the contents of her stomach roiled, and the next thing Shannon knew, she was running to the bathroom to vomit.

CHAPTER 15

*B*rian and William Knox strode into the sleek office of Robert Manchester, both of them ready to spit fire. Since they were actual fire witches, there was a distinct possibility of that reality coming true.

"Manchester," William Knox barked. "What is this nonsense about a lawsuit unless my son marries your daughter? Why in the bloody hell would you want a man who doesn't love her to put a ring on that finger?"

"Your son embarrassed her and our family," Robert barked back, using the exact same tone. It was as if they'd taken the same class in assholery. "He *will* do something to get her out of this mess, or we're going to have a major problem. I will not let my daughter be the laughing stock of Orange County."

Brian stood back with his arms crossed over his chest. It was like watching two roosters in a pen, preening before a cock fight. Egos like theirs were just one of the reasons he'd left LA and moved to Keating Hollow. He couldn't believe he'd been called back for something so incredibly stupid.

"Your daughter made up lies for an endorsement deal," William said. "Don't think I didn't find out about that six-figure payout she received for endorsing that bedding line. If you take this to court, that will come out. What do you think will happen when the court records show there never was any wedding? She'll be repaying that money, probably with some damages. Drop this, have your daughter issue a retraction, and we can all go back to taking care of business."

"She didn't lie." The short, balding CEO of Manchester Corp said as he stood and walked around the desk. He opened the glossy copy of *Cali Style* and flipped to the article in question. After clearing his throat, he said, "The direct quote is 'Yes, we've talked about marriage. I'm thinking a fall wedding.' What about that is false? We have talked about the two of them getting married. Multiple times. And Cara has always said she'd like to get married in the fall on the beach."

"The *we* in that sentence implies she's referring to my son, Manchester. You're talking semantics while I'm talking about integrity. We won't stand for this." William took a step closer and snagged the magazine out of Manchester's hands. "You and I both know she crossed a line. If you want to battle it out in the courts—"

Brian cleared his throat, already losing his patience. "This entire thing is ridiculous. I'll be issuing a statement to the press that we aren't engaged, that we never were, and that Cara and I have always merely been family friends. And I'll leave it at that. It implies the interviewer got it wrong, and we can all move on with our lives."

Manchester narrowed his eyes. "That is not how this is going to go down. For now, we'll do nothing. A few months from now, we'll leak that the engagement is off and that will be the end of it."

Brian briefly wondered if that might be the easiest option. He didn't give two figs what southern California society thought of him. If Shannon hadn't been a factor, he might have just said yes, gotten everything in writing, and left town without any intention of ever working with the bastard again. But he did have Shannon to consider. Or at least he had been close to having her before this fake news blew up in his face. And he fully intended to win back her trust. He couldn't do that if he had to lay low and act like she was someone he had to keep in the closet.

"I'm dating someone," Brian said. "I won't hide that, and I won't let your daughter insinuate that I was cheating either. So that scenario just isn't going to work for me."

"William," Manchester said, staring Brian's dad down with a pointed glare. "Talk some sense into your son. No one wants a scandal here. What's the big deal, anyway? So, he spends a few months laying low. This doesn't have to be such an ordeal."

Brian moved closer to Manchester, his body vibrating with anger now. "The only reason my father is here today is because you threatened a lawsuit against his company. He isn't here to negotiate on my behalf regarding what I will or won't do where your daughter is concerned. Got that? Whatever you have to say, you say it to me or not at all."

William Knox let out a tiny grunt of approval and said, "I think it's best if we dissolve the partnership we started, Robert. It's clear we don't share the same values. I'll have my lawyer draw up the necessary documents."

"You can't do that!" Manchester yelled, his face turning so red it appeared as if he might pop a blood vessel. "We have investors to answer to and projects in the works."

"You might have investors," William said, "but I don't. Or at least none that have actually put money down yet. This deal wasn't set in stone, and you know it. You're banking on the fact that you think we need this. We don't. There are other ways to achieve the same goal, other businesses that would love to partner with Knox Corp." He turned to his son. "Brian, you ready?"

Brian stared at his father, open-mouthed. He hadn't expected his dad to cut ties with the man completely. They'd known each other forever and had talked about this partnership for years. No matter what his father said, it would be a blow to the company to dissolve this venture now. The only possible reason William Knox was walking away was because he couldn't stomach working with Manchester after this interaction. Was it the way he'd treated Brian, or was it the threat of a lawsuit? William Knox hadn't gotten to be a top CEO by being a fool. Any man who impulsively threatened frivolous lawsuits was one who couldn't be trusted in business, no matter how long they'd known each other.

"I'm ready." Brian made eye contact with Manchester. "I'll give Cara until Saturday to set the record straight. If she doesn't, I'll be making my own statement."

"Saturday!" Manchester cried. He started to rant about needing more time and that Cara was heartbroken over the entire thing, but Brian ignored it all as he followed his father to the door. He would not be manipulated.

"You made your bed, and now you'll have to lie in it," Manchester called after them. "I hope you have plenty of money for legal fees because I'm going to fight the dissolution of the partnership with everything I've got, Knox! And your son is going down with you for services paid but never rendered."

Brian paused in the doorway of the man's office and

glanced back one last time. "Your deposit will be refunded to you by the end of the day, sir. Consider our contract null and void." Then he closed the door behind him and didn't say another word until his father pulled into the parking lot of the Knox Corporation building.

"Do you think you can get out of that partnership without any legal tangles?" Brian asked.

His father shrugged. "Maybe. Maybe not. I'll meet with legal as soon as I get back into my office."

Brian forced himself to not slump down in his seat like he was a sullen teenager. He hadn't done anything wrong here. There wasn't anything to feel guilty about. Even so, he hated that something related to his personal life was causing trouble with his father's business. "Is there anything I can do?"

His father barked out a laugh. "Yesterday I would've said to date Cara and see if you could make a match."

Brian bristled, ready to argue, but his father put his hand up, stopping him. "Today my advice is the exact opposite. Stay away from her and Manchester. They are both unstable. I don't know why I didn't see that side of Robert before. I guess I always admired his aggressive style in business dealings, but this is the first time I've seen him make it so personal. We will not be partners with someone like that."

The tension in Brian's neck eased, and he felt about ten pounds lighter than he had when he woke up that morning in his parents' house. There were still business consequences to worry about though. "How serious do you think he is about suing us?"

"It's probably not an idle threat, but he'll likely drop it when it gets close to actually being heard by a judge. This is just a tactic to see if he can get us to budge by costing us a lot of money. Don't worry about it. I'll put the Knox Corp legal team to work on it and have them cover any filings against Knox Designs as well."

Brian had expected his father to offer his resources. It would've been out of character for him not to. Robert Manchester wasn't the only CEO who was protective of his child. But Brian couldn't allow that. He was a grown man. He'd take care of his own issues. "Thanks, Dad. I appreciate that, but I can handle it."

William Knox raised both eyebrows at his son. "You don't want me to cover what is guaranteed to be a few years' worth of legal bills because my business partner tried to screw you?"

"When I left Knox Corp, I told you that I'd take care of myself. And I have. There's no reason to change that now."

His father let out a bark of laughter. "Stubborn mule. You're just like me. Now I know your company is going to be a huge success." His expression turned serious as he peered at his son. "Listen, Brian. I want you to know that I heard you. I took off on my own as a young man, too. There was no way I was going to let my old man help me. I wanted to prove myself, and I had to do it on my own two feet. I get it."

"But…" Brian said with a small laugh. "There's always a but."

"But I can't let you take on the cost of any legal action that is brought on by Robert Manchester. This is on me and your mother for pushing an issue we had no right to push. Let me take responsibility for that. Please."

Brian stared at his father for a long moment. Then he slowly nodded, understanding that this was his dad's way of apologizing to him. "All right. Thank you."

"No thanks necessary. Now let's go get lunch." His father

hopped out of the BMW and was waiting for him near the garage elevators by the time Brian caught up.

William Knox launched into a conversation about the latest marketing campaign for the hotels, and it was clear they were done discussing Robert and Cara Manchester.

CHAPTER 16

After lunch, Brian said goodbye to his father and went outside in the warm summer sun to wait for Cara. He'd promised he'd talk to her before he left town, but he'd also already ordered his Uber to the airport so the meeting would be cut short. There just wasn't that much to say. He was taking a seat on one of the sidewalk benches when Cara rushed up to him.

"Oh, thank goodness I didn't miss you," she gushed as she sat down next to him. She was out of breath and looked like she'd been running.

"Cara, I don't think we have much to talk about," he said, ice lacing his tone. "I've already told your father everything you need to know."

"I came to apologize." She stared up at him, her blue eyes doe-like. "I made a mistake, and I want to know if you can forgive me. I didn't mean to cause so many issues."

"You told the world that we were getting married when we weren't even dating," he all but yelled at her, already completely out of patience. Between the impromptu flight down to southern California and the meeting with her father, Brian was over the whole thing.

"Shh!" She glanced around warily and then bit down on her lower lip.

"I don't have to be quiet," he said. "I'm not the one who made up a story just to secure an endorsement deal."

She hung her head, not even trying to deny her actions. "It was a... mistake." Her head popped back up, and there were unshed tears standing in her eyes.

"Cara, I can't do this right now. My ride will be here soon." Brian stood and checked his phone to see when his ride would actually get there. *Dammit.* He'd have to endure her for another four minutes.

One tear fell down her cheek, and it was all he could do to not scream. This woman needed a therapist or something. She thrust a folded piece of paper at him. "Here. Look at this."

He let out a sigh but did as she asked just to pass the time. He unfolded it to find his own handwriting and a doodle of a cartoon man and woman getting married.

The text said: *To Cara, the pretty girl in art class. Since our parents seem determined to pair us off, how about we make a pact that if we aren't married by the time we're thirty-five we'll just marry each other. Circle one. Yes or No.*

The yes had been circled with a red marker, and there was a lip-shaped lipstick imprint below the handwriting.

Oh, hell. Brian was already thirty-six, and since she was a couple of years behind him, he supposed she was about to turn thirty-five. Why had he been such a flirt in high school? He'd completely forgotten about the note until that very moment. Obviously, it was just the high school shenanigans of a boy looking for attention. He distinctly recalled writing a couple of similar notes to a few other girls he'd known. One in junior high and one in college. At that age, he'd obviously liked having backup options.

"This was just a teenager's joke," Brian said gently, handing the paper back to her. The fact that she'd kept it all those years made Brian uneasy. Had she been carrying a torch for him since they were kids?

"I know," she said quietly. "It's just that our parents were going on about us getting married last time we were all together, and you made a joke about what our kids would look like. And I started thinking maybe it wasn't such a bad idea."

He'd made a joke about their kids? It was possible, he supposed. He often made jokes about things he found uncomfortable. And he'd always been uncomfortable with the family expectation and pressure to merge the two empires through marriage.

"Anyway, then this spring you said I could stay with you for Jacob's wedding and I... I had that interview shortly after we made those plans, and I was so sure we were finally going to start something this summer. I got completely carried away. I owe you an apology."

He stared down at her, completely stunned. The entire situation was so surreal.

"I know I sound crazy," she said, turning away from him. "I promise you I'm not going to turn into a stalker or anything. I just... I let my daydreams get away from me. I'm sorry."

"All right," he said quietly, not knowing what else to say. He wanted to demand she issue a retraction, call her father off, and then make sure she stayed the heck away from him and Keating Hollow. But he said none of those things because she was shaking like a leaf and he didn't want to cause her anymore pain. Instead, he held his arms out for her and folded her into a hug. "It's going to be all right, Cara. This will blow over, and one day no one will remember or care about it."

She let out an incredulous huff of laughter. "Yes, they will."

"No, I don't think so. Things are insane down here, and there's always a new story to latch onto. Next week by this time, another reality television star will have shoplifted something, and that will dominate the gossip sites."

Cara pulled back and looked up, giving him a small smile. "You're a good guy. You know that?"

"I try. But it gets me in trouble sometimes." He let her go and stuffed his hands back into his pockets.

"I will make this right, Brian," she said, staring at her feet again. "I just wonder if you could give me a few weeks before I make the announcement."

"I can't pretend to be your fiancé, Cara. I have someone in my life. I won't hide that. The press is already all over it, calling me a cheater and hounding her."

She grimaced. "Silas Ansell's sister. I know. I didn't mean to cause problems there."

"Well, you did. She won't return my phone calls right now." His voice was sharper than he'd intended, but there was no point in hiding how angry he was about this whole thing.

"I'm sorry." She closed her eyes and took a deep breath. "The only reason I asked is because I... um, need to make another announcement at the same time, and it will be really good publicity."

Was she really asking him for a favor after all the trouble she'd caused? "You can't be serious. So it's all about you again?" he asked, in a tone laced with both exhaustion and irritation. He glanced around for the Toyota Camry that was supposed to be picking him up.

"No, I..." She clamped her mouth shut and muttered

something to herself. "Right. I did just make it all about me. I'm sorry. It's— You know how this town is. All publicity is good publicity."

He disagreed and couldn't wait to get home away from the crazies. Then he eyed her, wondering exactly what she was up to. "What's the publicity for? Not another endorsement that is tied to the fake engagement, I hope."

This time she at least had the decency to flush when he called her out on her ridiculousness. "No. Nothing like that." She glanced around as if checking to make sure no one was listening. Then she lowered her voice and said, "I'm going to be on that reality show where people are locked in a house for ninety days with the cameras rolling twenty-four hours a day. My participation is still under wraps, and I'm not supposed to say anything just yet. But if I make an announcement that our engagement is broken right after the lineup comes out, it will really help me with the fans. I thought—"

"Holy shit," he muttered to himself. She was quite possibly insane. It also meant that perhaps she had a really good shot at winning the show. Not that he cared. He just wanted to go home. "Listen, Cara. Do whatever you want to do. I'm going home. I'm going to work things out with my girl. If the gossip blogs write about us, it is what it is. I'll make my announcement indicating we were never a couple whenever I feel like it. All right? I'll expect you to announce that we were never actually engaged and that we've gone our separate ways within two weeks. And if you can get your dad to back off the lawsuit, in return, I promise to never say anything else to the press. Deal?"

"Deal. I'm pretty sure I can make that work for me even if you do announce we aren't engaged." She beamed and held out her hand.

What did she mean by 'make it work'? His head started to ache, and he considered not shaking with her. He didn't even want to touch her. But he wanted a gentleman's agreement, so he took her hand, shook it, and then strode off to the Toyota Camry that had finally arrived to take him to the airport.

CHAPTER 17

"*I* think I might be dying," Shannon said as she slumped into one of the chairs at Incantation Café. "I can no longer feel my arms."

Silas sat across from her and promptly rested his head on the table, moaning about the ache in his back. "Never again. We should've hired movers. What were we thinking?"

"We were thinking that we don't have the cash on hand for movers right now," Shannon said irritably. She'd thought she'd been so clever with her money. She'd spent the past ten years diligently paying off her student loans while also funding her retirement. On paper, she was in great financial shape for a thirty-one-year old who managed a confectionary shop. She just didn't have a lot of *accessible* cash reserves at the moment.

That was a minor problem since she'd just put a first and last months' rent and a security deposit down on a small house three doors down from her grandmother's house. Or rather the house where her parents would no longer let her live rent free.

Silas would've gladly helped out. The kid had oodles of

money. But since he was underage, he only had access to a small amount each month. The rest had to be approved by their mother. When he turned eighteen, all of that would change.

"As much as my body aches right now, I'm still happy that Bellatrix left and went back to Los Angeles," Silas said, sitting up and stretching his legs out in front of him.

"You don't honestly think she's going to stay away, do you?" Shannon asked as she glanced over at Hanna, who was behind the register ringing up a couple of tourists.

"No. But she's gone for now, and that's all that matters," Silas said. He followed Shannon's gaze. "Rock, paper, scissors to see who has to get up and get us drinks?"

"My arms don't work, remember?" Shannon flexed her fingers and let out a groan. They'd moved Shannon's couch and overstuffed chair, her bedroom furniture, the dining room set, and the bar stools, along with a bunch of boxes of stuff Shannon had collected over the years. Since the house was only three doors down, they hadn't bothered to rent a truck. Again, another money saving move that they'd pay for when they couldn't even get out of bed in the morning.

"Too bad Brian wasn't in town. I bet he'd have moved everything for us," Silas said wistfully.

"We're not talking about him," Shannon said and sent Hanna an imploring look.

Hanna let out a loud laugh as she slipped out from behind the counter and made her way over to them. "You two look like you need someone to carry you out of here."

"Are you offering?" Shannon asked. "'Cause I wouldn't say no. But I do need a latte first. And a piece of coffee cake. Make that two pieces and the largest latte you can make. Double shot."

"Same," Silas said. "And water."

Hanna laughed. "Coming right up."

Shannon handed her a credit card. "Give yourself a thirty percent tip for waiting on our sad butts."

Hanna shook her head. "That's too much."

"No, it isn't. Forget it. I'll just write it on the receipt." Shannon smiled up at the gorgeous café owner. "Thanks again. I know we're a pain."

"No, you're not, and don't worry about it." Hanna pushed her dark curls out of her eyes and waved at someone as the door chimed.

Hope Scott strode into the café and up to the counter. After she ordered, she made her way over to Shannon and Silas. "Hey, kids. I hear you've had a rough day."

"Moved. It sucked," Silas said.

She nodded. "I've done far too much of that myself this past year. Although air magic usually helps. Did you run out of steam or something?"

"Shannon broke her wand about a half hour in, and after that everything went haywire," Silas grumbled.

"It's not like you were any help," she shot back. "If you ever practiced, you wouldn't be prone to dropping everything."

He raised both hands, palms up in a what-can-I-say motion, but then winced at his aching muscles.

"Wow. You two *are* in rough shape," Hope said. She eyed them. "You know, I do have a couple of openings at the spa tonight. Want to come in and let me work out those aches and pains?"

"Ugh," Silas groaned. "I'd love to, but Levi invited me over. Tomorrow?" He batted his best puppy-dog eyes at her.

She chuckled. "He finally decided to let you back in his bubble, huh?"

Silas's cheeks turned bright red as he glanced down at the table. "He's not thrilled about the tabloid articles."

"No. He isn't," Hope said, giving him a gentle smile. "But he also knows it's not something you have control over. So as long as you don't bring an entourage, I'm sure everything will work out."

"An entourage. Gods." He put his head back down. "Can't I just take the rest of the year off and live here in peace for a while?"

Shannon reached over and patted his hand. "It's probably better if you finish your obligation to *Timekeeper*. But whatever you want to do, I support you."

He turned his head and peered at her. When he spoke, his voice was full of hope. "Does this mean you've decided to be my manager?"

"Yes," she said with a sigh and rubbed at her forearms. "But I can't do that until your birthday."

"You can if I can convince Mom to let you start doing it sooner," he said, his eyes narrowing the way they did when he was calculating something in that sharp mind of his.

"Si, we don't need to rock the boat even more," Shannon said cautiously.

"Yes. Yes, we do." He suddenly stood and walked over to the counter to retrieve their order. His movements were smooth and confident.

"How is he doing that?" Shannon muttered. "I don't think I can even get out of this chair without pulling a muscle."

Hope cackled. "Youth. They bounce back faster."

"Not that fast." Shannon watched as Silas grabbed his drinks and pastries and then took off out the front door. Hey! Couldn't he at least have brought hers to the table before leaving? She was still scowling after him a moment later when

Hanna appeared with Shannon's half of the order and her credit card.

"Silas took care of the tip," Hanna said as she handed Shannon the receipt.

Shannon pursed her lips, studying the café owner. "You're not just saying that are you?"

"Nope." She pulled a twenty out of her pocket. "He wouldn't let me make change either."

Shannon felt pride well up inside her chest. Her brother was a good man. And considering he was raised by their parents, it was remarkable he'd turned out so kind. "Thanks, Hanna."

"Sure, sweetie. Now let Hope work out those achy muscles tonight so you can actually move tomorrow." She patted Shannon on the shoulder before heading back to the counter where Rex Holiday was standing with Rhys, Hanna's fiancé.

Rex's face lit up with a smile when he spotted Shannon. He said something to Rhys and then headed over. "Hey, ladies. How is your Friday night going?"

"Good," Hope said. "I'm on break before I go back to work."

Both of them turned their attention to Shannon. She let out a humorless laugh. "I've been better. I moved today and think I need a four-way limb transplant. Hope thinks she can save them with a massage."

"I'd trust Hope on this one," Rex said.

"You're probably right." Although Shannon was keenly aware that it was Friday evening, the night she and Brian were supposed to have their couple's massage. She still hadn't taken any of his calls. In fact, she'd blocked his number. Childish? Maybe. But she didn't think that any man who lied to her deserved her time.

Shannon could still hear Silas questioning if the story of

Brian's engagement was true though, and that unsettled her. Maybe she should have talked to him to at least hear what he had to say. She shook her head. Now wasn't the time to be mooning about Brian. Not when sexy Rex Holiday was standing in front of her. Shannon waved at the empty chair next to her. "Have a seat."

"I thought you'd never ask." Rex sat down next to her and immediately ran a gentle finger over the bruise on the back of her hand. "What happened here?"

"Banged it on the banister railing when my brother and I were hauling my mattress upstairs."

"And this?" His finger moved to a scrape on her forearm.

The connection was nice after a hard day of manual labor, but his touch was nothing like Brian's. She didn't feel any tingles or yummy shimmers of desire. *Dammit.* It sure would have been nice to be attracted to a guy who actually appeared to be available. She held back a disappointed sigh as she said, "I don't even know. I'm not sure I even felt it when I did that."

"I've been there before. Working on farms means I get all kinds of scrapes and bruises that I can't explain at the end of the day." He sat back in the chair and moved his hand to the table.

"How is it going at the Pelsh winery?" Shannon asked and then took a deep swig of her latte. The caffeine was like a shot in the arm, instantly perking her up.

"Good. They have a nice little vineyard out there."

Hanna arrived and grinned at him as she handed him his coffee. "It's only nice because we have a fabulous earth witch making sure we start off right."

"Thanks for that lovely compliment," he said, squeezing her hand lightly. "But your dad laid a fabulous groundwork before

I ever even knew the Pelsh vineyard existed. I don't think I could've asked for a better crop."

"That's what we like to hear." She glanced at Hope and Shannon. "Let me know if you need anything else."

"I'm good," Shannon said, raising her latte. "This is perfect." She turned her attention back to Rex. "Tell me more about the vineyard. What is it you do for the Pelshes, exactly?"

"I'm basically just tending the grapes, making sure the crop is in the best possible shape. The better it is in the beginning, the stronger it will be over time."

"So you're sort of like a consultant who comes in to get the place running in tiptop shape?" Hope asked, leaning in to give him her full attention.

"Something like that," Rex said. "It's going fantastic so far, but it will be even better when we find another air witch to help us get the vines tied up and work on aerating the wines."

"You need an air witch? I'm an air witch." Shannon said, leaning in closer. The muscles in her back screamed at her for moving, but she ignored the pain, keeping her full attention on Rex. He needed an air witch. She was an air witch. A second job would mean more money. Money that she'd need if she was going to try to buy her grandmother's house when it went on the market. The only issue would be what hours she had to work. She still had her manager job at A Spoonful of Magic after all. "Are there specific hours or are they flexible?"

His expression lit up with interest. "Flexible. Definitely. Are you interested?"

Shannon nodded. "I need a part time job."

"She's a talented air witch, too," Hope interjected. "If you've ever seen her wield that wand of hers, then you know what I'm talking about."

Wand. Right. She'd need to replace hers ASAP. Like by

tomorrow unless she wanted to go back to doing everything by hand. She wasn't good at direction when only using her fingers.

"Sounds perfect. Do you have time to come out to the vineyard tomorrow?" he asked.

Shannon leaned in, giving him her undivided attention. "If you're available in the afternoon, absolutely."

"I'll make sure I'm there." He reached out, offering her his hand.

Shannon took it and said, "I can't wait."

After Rex left with Rhys, Shannon turned to Hope. "Are you still available for that massage tonight?"

"Absolutely." Hope stood and gestured for Shannon to follow. "I was going to take walk-ins. You can be my first."

CHAPTER 18

Shannon's apprehension slammed into her as soon as she walked through the doors of A Touch of Magic. Why had she agreed to come here on Friday night? The night that was supposed to have been her and Brian's second date?

Right, she thought as she lowered herself into one of the chairs in the waiting room. She could barely move without wincing. This was one hundred percent for herself. She would not let thoughts of Brian ruin it for her.

As Hope went into the back to get her work area ready, Shannon flipped through a *Witch's Times* magazine and admired a new line of wands. There was a sparkly red one that just screamed her name.

"Shannon?" Lena, the spa's receptionist, called.

Shannon tossed the magazine on the table and winced when she pushed herself up. "I'm here."

"Oh, good. Right this way." Lena smiled at her and led her down the hall where the massage rooms were located. But instead of depositing her in one of the rooms, she kept going until they were out in the back garden.

Shannon spotted him right away. Brian was sitting at a table for two, candles lighting up his handsome face. A surge of irritation almost had her turning around and bolting back through the door. But Silas's words persisted in her mind, making her wonder what exactly he had to say about his supposed engagement. At the very least she deserved a little closure, right?

"Shannon?" Lena asked, frowning. "Is everything all right?"

Shannon cleared her throat. "I thought I was just getting a massage with Hope. This date was supposed to be canceled."

Lena's eyes widened, and then she glanced at Brian and back at Shannon. "Um, okay. If you want to follow me back into the spa, I can check with Hope and—"

Shannon waved a hand, stopping her. "No, never mind. That isn't necessary. Just please let Hope know I'm out here with Brian. As long as there is a massage for me by the end of the night, I'm fine."

"Of course," Lena said quickly. "I'm so sorry for the confusion."

"It's not your fault. Thanks, Lena."

Shannon took her time walking the rest of the distance to the table where Brian sat waiting for her. When she finally got there, she paused and placed her hand on the back of the empty chair. "I didn't think you'd be here."

"Of course I'm here. We had a date," he said, getting up and pulling her chair out for her.

She hated that he was so chivalrous. It made it harder for her to hate him. And at that moment, she was pretty sure she did hate him. Or at the very least, she hated how he'd made her feel and that she was actually going to sit down and let him explain. Did that make her weak? A bad feminist? Maybe. Maybe not. She pushed the destructive thoughts out of her head and sat back in her chair with her arms crossed over her chest.

"Did you get any of my texts?" Brian asked when he was seated across from her again.

She shook her head. "It's been a rough week. I ended up blocking you."

Pain flashed in his dark eyes for just a moment before he nodded slowly. "I understand."

"Do you?" she challenged. "I'm not sure you really have any idea what it's like to find out the guy you just started dating is engaged." There. She'd said it.

Brian took a deep breath and nodded. "You're right. I don't. But can you imagine getting a phone call first thing in the morning and learning you're engaged to someone you've never actually dated?"

Shannon stared at him as if he had two heads. Had she heard him correctly? Was he trying to say that even he didn't know about the engagement? That seemed... far-fetched at best. Or was it? Silas had warned her about the press. She just hadn't considered that he might be right. "Care to explain that?"

"Are you ready to hear it?" he asked. There wasn't any challenge in his voice, just a gentle curiosity.

Dammit if that wasn't endearing. "I think so." She sucked in a breath and let it out. "Listen. My brother is a major star. I spent some time in Hollywood when I was in college. I understand how crazy it can be down there. I also know that people tend to exaggerate the truth or just make up lies to get what they want. I'm willing to listen, but if you're not truthful and I find out, there won't be another chance. Understand? I hate drama. I hate the press. And most of all, I hate liars."

"Then we have more in common than I realized, Shannon,

because I feel exactly the same way." This time when he smiled at her, it was full of all his charm, and he seemed as if he was amused. Like she'd said something that delighted him.

"All right then. Lay it on me." She picked up the flute of champagne that was sitting in front of her and took a sip.

Brian leaned forward, propping his elbows on the table. "It's pretty crazy. Are you ready for this?"

"I doubt it. But it's been a crazy week, so go for it. It can't be worse than my own mother kicking me out of my house." Oops. She hadn't meant to say that. She didn't want to give him any details of her week until she heard what he had to say.

He lifted one eyebrow, the one that had a scar running through it. She briefly wondered how that had happened and made a note to ask him later. "We're definitely coming back to that."

She shrugged one shoulder, ignoring the pain, and waited. The candlelight around him made his skin glow, and she hated herself for noticing. She shouldn't be warming to him already. He hadn't even explained himself yet.

"Cara Manchester is the daughter of one of my father's oldest friends. Or at least they were friends until a few days ago. They were also going into business together. Manchester and Knox Corps. Hotels and spas. Big business."

"Okay," Shannon said, frowning. "So what? This is one of those arranged, empire-building marriages?"

Brian laughed, but there wasn't any humor in it. "Sort of? For years our families have made comments about how I should marry Cara. I always made a joke out of it because their pressure made me uncomfortable. I have never had any intention of dating or marrying Cara. In fact, she's a crazy Hollywood type, and I couldn't be more turned off if I tried. There is nothing there."

"So why did she think there was going to be a wedding happening next fall?" Shannon asked, her curiosity getting the better of her patience.

This time his laugh was bitter. "She didn't really think that. It was all a lie, a publicity stunt for an endorsement deal and a reality television show she's been booked on."

Shannon sat back in her chair, stunned. When she finally found her voice, she said, "That sounds like one incredible story, Brian."

"I know. But it's the truth." He picked up his champagne flute and downed the contents. "I had to go down there and deal with her father, who is concerned about his daughter being a laughing stock. He and my dad are threatening each other with lawsuits, because after the way old man Manchester behaved, my dad wants nothing to do with him. It's a right mess and exactly why I left Knox Corp. I have no interest in all that drama. I just want a quiet life here in Keating Hollow where I get to babysit Skye and set my own hours. And start dating you, if you're game."

Shannon stared at Brian, shock rendering her speechless. His story was incredible. And yet, she one hundred percent believed him. It was just the type of crazy she'd run from ten years ago. It was the same type of crazy her mother had brought to her front door earlier in the week.

"Shannon?" Brian asked. "Are you all right? You look a little—"

She threw her head back and burst out laughing. She couldn't help it. How was it possible they were living exactly the same life only with different details? "Oh hell, Brian. I'm sorry. I'm not laughing at you. I promise."

"Are you sure?" he asked as she continued to chuckle.

"Wait until you hear what happened with my mother."

Shaking her head, she wiped at her eyes that were watering from her hysterics. She then explained how Gigi Ansell was trying to run Silas's life and had stooped to blackmail when Shannon had been unwilling to help her.

"So she kicked you out of your grandmother's house because you wouldn't take her side on what Silas should do with his career?" Brian asked.

"Oh, no, Brian. It isn't Grandma's house. It's *her* house. Or at least that's what she says. Technically, Grandma left the house to my dad, but he does whatever she says, so that detail hardly matters."

"That's... cold." His eyes were suddenly stormy, angry on her behalf, and it made her smile.

"Hey," she said, reaching across the table to cover his hand with her own. "It's okay. My mom and I haven't seen eye to eye for years. All I want is to make sure that Silas is all right. She's causing all kinds of problems for him right now. It's making him miserable, and I'm afraid he's going to tank his career if she doesn't let up."

"Like you did?" He twined his fingers between hers.

"Nah. I liked acting, but never enough to put up with the BS. Silas loves what he does. I just don't want her to ruin it for him."

"She won't," he said.

"How do you know?"

"Because you won't let her." Brian squeezed her fingers, giving her reassurance. "Silas knew what he was doing when he came here. You're the one person he can rely on."

He was right. Shannon was the only one in her brother's life who cared solely about him and what he wanted. She was his rock. And always would be. No way was she going to let him down now.

"Thanks for that," Shannon whispered, glancing down at their joined hands. She couldn't help thinking, *Damn, that feels good.* The crushing disappointment that had been weighing on her ever since she saw that article online was gone. Her heart was lighter and so was her spirit. For the first time in days, she actually felt like she could breathe. And it was all because she'd fallen for him.

CHAPTER 19

The ache in Brian's gut had finally eased. The moment Shannon had smiled at him and then let him hold her hand, the wariness of the last few days had finally faded away. The fact that she hadn't answered any of his texts had bothered him, but when she said she'd blocked his number, he was certain he'd missed his chance. But by some stroke of luck, she managed to put the gossip behind her, behind them, and was clearly having fun in the moment.

"Here, try this." Brian held a forkful of his lobster risotto out to her for her to try. And when her lips wrapped around the utensil, he thought he'd pass out right there. What he wouldn't give to have those lips on his... and other places.

"Why are you looking at me like that?" she asked with a seductive gaze, as if she knew exactly what was going through his mind.

"I was just thinking about the massages waiting for us." The image of her naked and lying beside him, even if it was on a massage table five feet away, was driving him insane. He had no idea how he was going to survive an hour, knowing she was right there but unable to touch her. Couple's massage suddenly seemed like a very bad idea.

"I think maybe we should have had the massages first, then dinner," Shannon mused. "I'm probably going to fall into a food coma and miss half of it."

He agreed but knew there was no way that was going to happen to him. His body was too attuned to hers. If he hadn't known she was so sore from moving, he might've suggested skipping the massages at the spa and offered to do the honors himself. But it was way too soon. She'd just started talking to him again.

Down, boy, he ordered himself and took another drink of champagne.

"Your risotto is going to get cold," she said, her eyes sparkling with mischief.

"Who cares?" he replied, staring her down like she was his next bite.

"Okay, dude. I get it. You're ready for the massage portion of the evening. Should we flag down our waiter and let them know we're—"

A loud crash, followed by screaming and shouts, came from the front of the spa. Brian was out of his chair first with Shannon right behind him. He glanced over his shoulder and noticed her grimace as she rushed to keep up with him. Damn, she really was aching. He wanted to slow down for her, but instinct had him rushing to the lobby area of the building.

Faith Townsend stood in the middle of a pile of shattered glass, staring out the hole where her window used to be while she barked into the phone. "Drew? We have an issue. How soon can you get here?"

"Holy hell, Lena!" Shannon said from behind him. "What happened?"

Brian glanced back and saw Shannon holding her hand to her throat as she glanced around with wide eyes.

"Someone threw a brick through the window," Lena said, her voice shaking.

Brian vibrated with energy. The need to do something pulsed in his veins, and standing there waiting for the sheriff was out of the question. "Shannon, check to make sure Lena is all right. I'm going to check outside and see if anyone needs help."

Shannon grabbed his hand, stopping him. "I don't think you should go out there until Drew gets here."

He leaned down and brushed a kiss over her forehead. "I'll be fine. Trust me." Without another word, he stepped out of the spa and was nearly blinded by flash bulbs. He threw his hands up and turned away, trying to recover from the big bright spots swimming in his vision.

"Brian!" a man shouted. "Was anyone hurt? Are you bleeding?"

"Mr. Knox, can you tell us what your fiancée thinks of you having dinner with Ms. Ansell?"

"Is the wedding still on?"

"Does the brick that sailed through the window have anything to do with Cara Manchester?"

The questions bombarded him from every angle. How many reporters had been camped out in front of the spa? One of them must've seen something, right? He raised his arms, waving them in the air, trying to get everyone to quiet down.

But the questions kept coming along with the flash bulbs, and finally he gave up and went back inside to find everyone just staring at him. There was no reason to say anything. They'd all heard the questions. He walked over to Shannon, and without a word he pulled her into a hug. "Are you all right?"

She wrapped her arms around him but shook her head. "Not at all. Are we going to be able to get out of here without being mobbed?"

"I don't know," he said into her hair.

Shannon pulled back and turned to Faith. The pretty blonde had just returned from retrieving a broom and looked like she was ready to start cleaning up.

Lena stopped her though. "Not yet, Faith. We need to take pictures for the insurance. And Drew will want pictures for the police report."

"Right." She propped the broom against the wall and scanned the area, grimacing at the shattered vase and the shelf of merchandise that had been destroyed.

"Faith?" Shannon said.

"Yeah?" The spa owner appeared shaken, and Brian wondered if she'd already called her fiancé, Hunter. Probably not. He pulled his phone out of his pocket and called Jacob. He didn't have Hunter's number, but Faith's sister Yvette likely did. He spoke quietly, letting Jacob know what had happened, including the mob of paparazzi.

After Jacob relayed the information to his wife for her to call Hunter, he said, "Jeez, man, that's insane. Do you think they are camped out at your house, too?"

"Well, now I do." He ran a hand through his hair and felt like he wanted to come right out of his skin. How was he going to live like this for two more weeks before Cara got around to setting the record straight? He couldn't. He'd issue his own statement, but he knew no one would pay much attention to it until Cara responded. Cheating was just too good a scandal to ignore.

Maybe he should leave Keating Hollow and hide out for a bit. He glanced at Shannon and knew he couldn't leave her in this mess. He'd take her with him in a heartbeat, but who was to say the photographers wouldn't follow them? Especially if Silas was with them. It was a no-win situation.

"You can come here and use the guest room if you want," his friend said and then chuckled as he added, "Or share with Skye."

"That sounds restful," Brian said dryly. "I'll probably be there in a few hours after I get Shannon home safely."

"All right, man," Jacob said. "I'll leave a light on for you."

"Thanks." He ended the call and went to see what he could do to help.

An hour later, Drew had cleared the paparazzi, telling them all he needed them at the station for questioning and if they didn't comply, he'd haul them in himself.

"Thanks, man." Brian held his hand out to the deputy sheriff. "You have no idea how much that helps."

"I'm sorry they keep hounding you, Brian," Drew said, shaking his hand. "It's not something we're used to around here."

"No kidding. It's one of the reasons I moved here." He patted Drew on the shoulder and moved past him to collect Shannon. When he found her in one of the reception room chairs, he sat beside her and took her hand in his. "Ready to go?"

"Yes. You have no idea." She looked like she was dead on her feet, and after the day she'd had, he wasn't surprised.

"In that case..." Brian scooped her up and held her against his chest as he carried her outside to his SUV. She chuckled and told him carrying her wasn't necessary, but he noticed she didn't protest too hard.

"You're sweet. You know that, Brian Knox?" she said from the passenger seat.

Brian glanced over at her before starting the vehicle and felt a wave of tenderness wash over him as he stared into her whiskey-colored eyes. He couldn't stop himself from wanting to wrap her in his arms and keep her there forever. Which was ridiculous, because if ever there was a woman who could take care of herself, it was Shannon Ansell.

"Are you going to kiss me, or just stare at me all night?" she asked as her lips twitched with amusement.

"I will. Just give me a moment." He leaned over and cupped her cheek, savoring the way she was looking at him. Her expression was sleepy but full of love, and trust, and something that felt an awful lot like home. "I can't wait until the day I can hold you all night, Shannon."

Her breath caught, and she whispered, "Me neither."

"But not tonight. You need your rest," he continued.

"I can sleep while you cuddle me," she said with a tiny pout.

Brian laughed. "Nope. Not even close, gorgeous girl. I won't be able to keep my hands still."

She visibly shuddered at his words, and it only made him regret his decision to not take her home with him even more. Although, he wasn't going home, was he? He didn't know yet, but he'd place bets there were a bunch of photographers clogging his driveway at that very moment. "Fine, then kiss me already."

He felt his insides light up as his lips brushed over hers. And in that moment, everything was perfect.

CHAPTER 20

erfect. It was the word Brian had uttered right after that amazing kiss Shannon had shared with him in his SUV right outside of A Touch of Magic. But there wasn't anything perfect about Shannon's reality at the moment. She was supposed to be spending her first night away from her grandmother's home—the home she'd come to think of as her own—in her new rental, but instead, she was sitting in Brian's SUV, staring at the circle of photographers camped out on her sidewalk. "I can't stay there. Not after what happened at Faith's spa."

"Definitely not," Brian said. "You can come back to my place if you want."

There wasn't any innuendo or flirtation in his tone, only concern. She frowned and pressed a hand to her throbbing head. "Don't you think they'll be there, too?"

"Probably. Jacob already said I could use his spare room. I'm sure they won't mind one more guest if you want to come along."

"I could go to Noel's inn, I suppose," Shannon said, but she quickly dismissed the idea. "Only I bet some of these jerks are staying there."

"Probably," Brian agreed.

There weren't that many places to stay in Keating Hollow if you weren't already someone's personal guest. Shannon pulled out her phone and called Hope. After explaining the situation, Hope confirmed that Silas was still there with Levi and that the paparazzi were nowhere to be seen.

"You can stay here if you want," Hope said. "Levi's room is free. He's been staying downstairs while his ankle heals."

"That would be great. Thanks. See you in five." She ended the call and asked Brian if he could drop her off at Hope and Chad's place.

"Yeah, okay," he said, sounding slightly disappointed. But he gave her a tiny smile and put the SUV in gear.

Shannon stared out the window at the pretty tree-lined street and idyllic cottages and said, "I just don't understand why anyone would throw a brick through the spa's window. What did that accomplish?"

Brian let out a humorless laugh. "It got me outside, didn't it? They got their photograph. Only they couldn't have known I'd be the one to go out there, so I really don't have any idea. It seems random, doesn't it? The paparazzi doesn't usually resort to destruction of property."

"No. They don't. Usually stuff like that only happens when celebrities snap and an altercation takes place. I just don't get it."

"It feels like the world has gone crazy," Brian said.

"Not the entire world," Shannon said with a sigh. "We still have good friends who are there for us when we need them." As she heard herself say the words, a weird sense of peace settled over her. Shannon hadn't ever really felt like she fit in anywhere. She'd had Miss Maple all these years and Wanda, but Wanda was such a social butterfly that they didn't get a lot of quality time together. There were other residents of Keating Hollow she was friendly with, but until Hope arrived, she'd never really felt like she had a girlfriend she could count on. Nor a boyfriend for that matter. She'd dated of course, but no one had ever meant enough to make her want to stick with the relationship.

That had changed when Brian came into her life. She watched him from her side of the vehicle. His features were hidden in shadows, but she could still see his angular jaw and five o'clock shadow. Her fingers itched to touch his cheek, his lips, his soft hair. The man was beautiful; there was no doubt about it. And she suddenly regretted not taking him up on his offer to go back to Yvette and Jacob's house.

"What are you thinking about over there?" he asked, his voice husky.

She chuckled. "Nothing."

He turned and his smoldering gaze met hers. Yeah, he knew what she'd been thinking about, or at least guessed, and he was thinking the exact same thing. Her body warmed, and sweat broke out on the back of her neck.

"Is it hot in here or is it just me?" she asked, lowering the window a crack.

"You're definitely hot, Shannon."

She felt her cheeks heat as she flushed. "Stop. This conversation is only going to frustrate us both."

He laughed. "You could always change your mind you know."

She'd been considering it, if only subconsciously. But the truth was, she needed to be with Silas. If the paparazzi was going to keep coming for them, he needed to be her first priority. "I wish I could, but my brother..." She shrugged. "This kind of crap is really wearing on him. I need to stick close."

"I get it." He pulled into the driveway of the cottage Hope and Chad shared. The front porch light was on, illuminating the pretty red shutters. He reached over and cupped her cheek with his palm. "Can I call you tomorrow?"

She leaned into him, closing her eyes. "You better."

"Count on it." He gave her a slow, tender kiss and she prayed that the photographers would find a more interesting target as soon as possible. She wasn't sure she could take even another day without him in her bed.

Finally, Shannon broke away and hurried out of the SUV. Once she made it onto the porch, she turned and blew him one last kiss.

BRIAN SAT in the middle of the nursery floor, unable to forget the kiss Shannon had sent him once she hopped out of the SUV the night before. It had smacked him right in the chest, traveled down his limbs, and made his fingers and toes tingle with her magic. Shannon Ansell had sent him a magical kiss that he'd still be feeling for days to come. It had taken a long time to get to sleep the night before, and even then he was sure he dreamed about her.

Damn. Did he have it bad for Shannon Ansell or what?

The little girl running around him in the room let out a loud giggle, pulling him out of his Shannon haze. He laughed as Skye shoved a pink bear at him and went to work on attaching little pink and blue bows to his hair. She was wearing a green tutu and pink tights as she wiggled around, practicing the moves she'd learned in her toddler's Mommy and Me ballet class.

"Looks good, Skye," he said, holding a blue plastic mirror up to see his reflection. "You'll make a great stylist when you're older."

The toddler giggled, dropped her brown and white stuffed dog into his lap, and continued to hum while she added more bows to his hair.

"Lookin' good, man," Jacob said, chuckling from the doorway. "Are you just about ready for your photoshoot? I bet the paparazzi would pay big bucks for one of these shots."

"Dude, don't be a jack... um, jackhole. Don't be a jackhole." Brian leaned over and smacked a kiss on Skye's cheek. "Don't listen to Daddy. He's just jealous he doesn't have enough charisma to really rock this look."

Skye held up a pink bow to her father.

He took it and managed to attach it to a short lock in the middle of his head. Grinning at his daughter, he bent down so she could see his handiwork. "What do you think? Cute, right?"

"Cute!" she agreed and toddled off into the hallway.

Jacob watched her for a moment and then grinned. "Looks like someone was hungry." He turned his attention back to Brian. "She found Yvette. They're having breakfast now."

Brian nodded. He'd gotten up early and heard Skye singing to herself, so he'd come in to keep her entertained until Yvette and Jacob woke up. "She's growing so fast, Jay."

"Don't I know it. Next thing I know she's gonna be asking to borrow uncle Brian's SUV." He chuckled. "Or asking uncle Bri to buy her a pink convertible."

Brian laughed. "I'd do it, too. That girl is gonna be a fashion diva."

"Probably." He reached up and pulled the pink bow out of

his hair, dropping the accessory into the plastic bin next to Brian. "I'm making eggs and bacon. You in?"

"As long as there's coffee," Brian said, collecting the toys Skye had been playing with and dropping them in the trunk against the wall.

"Dude. There's always coffee." Jacob disappeared down the hall just as Brian's phone started to ring.

"Knox," he said when he didn't recognize the number.

"Brian? It's Drew Baker."

"Good morning, Drew," he said. "Do you have news about last night?" He couldn't imagine why else the deputy sheriff would be calling him.

"I do. We've got the suspect in custody, but I wanted you to be aware of the situation before it hits the news."

"Lay it on me," Brian said with more bravado than he actually felt. He walked out of Skye's room and down the hall where he could hear Yvette singing to Skye. He bypassed the kitchen and walked out onto the porch that looked out over the Keating Hollow valley. There were redwood trees for miles, and when the fog burned off, one could follow the curve of the river almost all the way to the coast.

"The suspect who threw the brick through the window at A Touch of Magic runs an online gossip site. She's been ranting online about you and your relationships with Cara Manchester as well as Shannon. She apparently believes that you cheated on Cara, and this suspect tried to take it upon herself to make you pay for your actions."

"What? You can't be serious. Cara and I weren't even an item," Brian said, realizing that Drew likely didn't care one way or another who Brian was dating or engaged to. All he cared about was keeping his residents safe.

Drew cleared his throat. "That's irrelevant. What matters is that Ms. Boxer feels that Cara has been wronged and has been making online threats against you and Shannon. Ms. Boxer has been booked, and we're collecting the evidence now."

"Shannon, too?" Brian asked, feeling sick. "Has anyone tried to hurt her?"

"No one has physically threatened Shannon... yet," Drew said. "But we're keeping a close eye on her. The stuff we found online is pretty disturbing." Drew paused and took a breath. "Listen, Brian. I'm not trying to worry you. I just want you and Shannon to be informed. I'll be calling her as soon as we're done here."

Brian felt sick at the idea that Shannon might be in danger because of him. It never should've happened. He wanted to rant and rave and punch something, but none of that would help. All he could really do was keep his distance until Cara set the record straight. He'd have to do what he could to speed that up. "I understand. Will you keep me updated with what happens to Ms. Boxer?"

"We will. Try not to worry too much about this. We're taking the situation seriously."

What was Brian supposed to say to that? How could he not worry? He'd hate himself if anything happened to Shannon or her brother. Or anyone else for that matter. That brick could've killed someone if anyone had been sitting in the chairs near the window.

"Brian?" Drew asked. "Are you still with me?"

"Yeah. I'm here. Listen, how did she know where to find us? Do you know? Shannon and I were eating dinner when the incident happened. We'd been there a while."

"She had an impressive amount of notes about you and Shannon in her vehicle, including your license plate numbers and your addresses."

"That's… disturbing," Brian said, feeling nauseated by the fact that someone was stalking not just him, but Shannon, too.

"It is, and that's why we're taking this very seriously," Drew said.

Drew's answer did nothing to reassure him. But he trusted the guy, so he just said, "Thanks for the call, man."

"Of course. Don't hesitate to let me know if you see anything suspicious."

After Brian ended the call with Drew, he scrolled through his contacts and pulled up his father's number.

When William Knox answered, Brian said, "Dad, I need a good publicist."

An hour later, he emailed the publicist a statement that denied a romantic involvement with Cara Manchester or the existence of any engagement. She assured him it would hit all the gossip sites no later than the next morning.

CHAPTER 21

"Shannon? Are you all right?" Silas asked.

She glanced up from her spot on the porch swing to find him standing next to the back door holding two coffee mugs. She'd escaped to the backyard when she answered her phone to speak to Drew when he called. And then she'd been gutted when she learned she was the target of an online gossip blog. She leaned back in the swing and shook her head. "Um, no. Not really."

Silas sat down on the swing next to her and handed her one of the mugs. "What did the deputy sheriff say?"

"Thanks," she said, nodding at the mug. Then she took a deep breath and relayed the information. "I'm basically the target on a hateful gossip blog for something I didn't do."

Her brother gave her a sympathetic smile. "I know how awful that is. But try to remember that ninety-nine percent of the time it's all talk."

Shannon frowned and gave Silas an irritated glance. "Except this crazy has already tried to hurt people. She threw a brick through Faith's window, remember?"

"You're right. Sorry." He rubbed the sleep out of his eyes and sighed. "At least the site owner is in custody. Maybe the outrage will calm down with their ringleader in jail."

"Maybe, but what's to stop one of the other hateful people from trying to take up where she left off?" Shannon asked. She knew she was spiraling and being slightly irrational about the possibility of a repeat attack. Silas was right. Most people were all talk and no action.

"No one in the public eye is ever immune to stalkers. You know that, Shan," Silas said gently. "But it probably helps that Keating Hollow is a small town where everyone looks out for each other. And Sheriff Drew seems like a decent guy from what Levi has told me."

"He is." Shannon took a long sip of her coffee that her brother had managed to doctor perfectly, just the way she liked it. She glanced around at the pretty backyard and said, "Do you think I could convince Hope to put a pool in? I miss ours."

Silas laughed. "If you're willing to pay for it and the upkeep, then probably."

"I guess I'll just have to start swimming in the river." One of Shannon's favorite things about her grandmother's house was the pool out back. In the summer, she used it all the time to both relax and get some exercise. But now that their mother had kicked them out, there wouldn't be any more swimming. Shannon was almost more bitter about that than anything else.

"At least you can control the temperature," Silas mused, referring to her ability to heat water with her air magic. Her brother did a good job of chatting about anything and nothing for the next hour until it was time for her to go to work.

"Thanks, Si," she said, giving him a hug.

"For what?" he asked.

"For calming me down. The talk. Just being normal so that

neither of us had to think about insane people bringing crazy into our lives. It was just what I needed this morning."

He stood and gave her a hug. "I've been there, sis. Now go to work and make that money."

She let out a snort. "I'm on it."

"RED OR PURPLE?" Shannon asked herself as she stood in front of a display of wands. The red one caught her eye right away. It was sleek and shiny and the perfect shade of what she referred to as whore red. But the purple one sparkled. And oh, how she loved it when her wand sparkled.

"Maybe both? You could have one as a spare," the clerk said.

Shannon raised one eyebrow at the owner of Wands and Things. The shop was a few doors down from A Spoonful of Magic, and Shannon had popped in quickly before she opened the confectionary shop. "A backup? Do people usually do that? Mine always gets better and more powerful the more I use it. The only reason I'm here now is because I broke the last one."

The clerk started to launch into something about never being caught with your pants down without a wand, and Shannon wondered briefly if she'd walked into a sex shop that sold some sort of kinky version of wands. But no. One look around the shop and it was definitely a standard magic supply store. She was giggling to herself when her phone buzzed.

A picture of Brian flashed on the screen, and she answered while still chuckling to herself. "Hey, you. I was hoping to hear from you soon."

"Hey yourself." His tone was somber, much more subdued than usual. Drew had told her he'd spoken with Brian, so he was probably still trying to process the previous night's events.

Desperate to get away from the clerk, who was still listing the benefits of backup wands, she grabbed the sleek red one and took it to the counter. As she paid the man working the register, she spoke into the phone, "Are you doing okay?"

"Not really," Brian said. "Did you talk to Drew?"

"I did." All of her amusement vanished, and she felt a crushing weight of guilt for what might have happened at Faith's spa if that brick had actually hit anyone. "I'm devastated and mortified to be honest, but I could not be more grateful that no one was hurt."

"I feel the same," Brian said, his voice suddenly hoarse. He cleared his throat, but it didn't help. His tone was still raspy when he said, "I think we should stop seeing each other."

She felt like she'd been punched in the stomach. The air whooshed out of her, and she couldn't get any words out.

"Here you go, ma'am. Have a nice day." The clerk handed over her wand and smiled at her as if Brian hadn't just ripped her heart out.

She nodded in return and rushed out of the shop.

"Shannon?" Brian said. "Are you still there?"

"Yes," she breathed as she unlocked the front door of A Spoonful of Magic. "I'm just getting to work."

"Oh. Okay. Did you want to call me back?" He sounded more normal now and it irritated her.

"No. I don't want to call you back. I want you to tell me why you're dumping me." The words flew out of her mouth before she could even think them through.

"I'm not. I swear I'm not dumping you." He paused. "I just think it would be safer for you, for everyone, if I laid low for a while until this Cara business blows over. I don't want anyone to get hurt."

Was he referring to someone's physical or mental

wellbeing? It was hard to tell considering the way he was going about this. "I don't either," Shannon said.

He let out a breath as if he was relieved that she agreed with him. "Right. Okay, so... Dammit. I'm sorry, Shannon. I'm doing this all wrong."

She leaned against the counter and said, "Yeah. This call is a little rough."

"I'm sorry. I just meant to say that I don't want to cause trouble for anyone and least of all you. I'm worried. And I think if we stay out of the public eye, don't give anyone anything to write about until Cara releases her statement to the press, then hopefully this will blow over quickly and we won't have another incident like last night."

"Okaaaay. When is Cara supposed to release this statement?" Shannon asked.

"Sometime in the next two weeks," Brian said, his tone full of bitterness. "But I just sent my father's publicist a statement. It should be out by tomorrow."

"No one will pay attention to that," Shannon said. "Not the ones who are already riled up, anyway."

"I know, but I had to put it out there. Then I'm done with it. Truly done."

She could hear how upset he was and could only imagine the guilt he felt about Faith's shop, so she decided to cut him a break. "You're right. Let's put the brakes on whatever this is and see where we're at when the paparazzi leaves town."

He groaned.

"What? That's what you said you wanted." Shannon said.

"It's what I think we should do. It's not what I want. Not at all. And you're still my date for Faith and Hunter's wedding a couple of weeks from now. Got that? I'm not giving up on that bet." His flirty tone was back, and she couldn't help but melt a little. "Not when there's a naked massage in it for me."

She laughed. "Of course you aren't. All right, fine. It will give us something to look forward to. But don't be a stranger. My phone works just fine. Call me, okay?"

Brian chuckled into the phone as he said, "Count on it, gorgeous."

CHAPTER 22

"This is beautiful," Shannon said as she walked through the Pelshes' vineyard. It was late afternoon, and the sun was low in the sky, casting a soft light over the vines that took her breath away. "You must be in heaven working here every day."

Rex grinned. "It's not a bad life."

"I can see that."

"Let me show you the barn where we do the bottling." He jerked his head toward a large structure that looked more like a ranch house than a barn.

Shannon followed him, noting how the afternoon sun highlighted his sun-bleached hair and tanned skin. She couldn't help but compare him to a surfer. He had that beach bum look about him. He just glowed and he had muscles for days. He had to work out. There was no way he was that fit simply from working the vineyard. Still, even though he was one really good-looking man, she couldn't help but wish she was with Brian instead. After their phone call that morning, all she could think about was driving over to his house and wrapping her arms around him.

"How's Brian?" Rex asked as if he could read her mind. "I heard what happened at the spa last night. Is he doing okay? I haven't had a chance to talk to him yet."

The good mood she'd managed to achieve vanished, but she didn't blame Rex. He was only concerned about his friend. "He's all right, I guess. Shaken up about the stalking and being indirectly responsible for what happened to Faith's window. He's just trying to lay low until the media storm dies down and the paparazzi gets bored and leaves town."

Rex winced. "Man, that sounds rough."

"It is."

Rex stopped at the front door of the barn and said, "That's right. Your brother has to deal with this stuff from time to time, too. It must be exhausting."

She took a deep breath and let it out. "It can be, but it really doesn't happen that often. Only when someone stirs the drama." She pasted on a smile. "But enough of that. Show me your operation. I'm dying to see how I can help."

"You got it," he said brightly, seeming to understand that she didn't want to talk about their problems. Rex was nothing but an excited earth witch as he showed her where they fermented the wine, where it was processed and aerated, and then where they kept the barrels while it aged. "We'd want you to help us aerate the batches. Did you bring your wand?"

Shannon whipped out her brand-new, whore-red wand and grinned. "Isn't she gorgeous?"

He laughed. "She?"

"Sure. Who else would wear this color?" She gave him an exaggerated wink and waved her wand with a flourish, sending a puff of air at him that ruffled his hair.

"Perfect. Let's see what you've got."

Shannon spent a half hour whipping up enough wind to aerate a couple of large batches of wine. By the time she was done, she was sweating and a little winded herself. "Wow, that was kind of a workout."

"That was impressive," Rex said with a nod. "You're going to be a fantastic asset to this team."

"Does that mean I'm hired?" she asked, really excited about the opportunity. She couldn't believe how much she loved the place. From the scenery, to using her air magic to create something, to the fresh-earth scent of the vineyard, she couldn't get enough.

"Definitely. When can you start?"

"Today?" she said with a laugh.

Rex chuckled. "Excited much? You really like it here, don't you?"

"I do. It's different, and I like being challenged," she said, leaning against one of the stainless steel counters. "Don't get me wrong, I love managing A Spoonful of Magic, but I've been doing that a long time. Most days I'm completely on autopilot."

"I fear that will happen here, too. It's mostly just tending vines and aerating the wine during the fermenting process," Rex said.

"That works. If I get bored, I'll have that incredible view to entertain me." She turned and looked out the window just in time to see the sun setting over the mountain. "Look, Rex. It's magic."

"It sure is," he said from right behind her, and she thought she heard a hint of longing in his tone. But when she glanced back to see his expression, he was already moving away from her toward the door. "Ready? It's quittin' time."

"Sure." She tucked her wand away and followed him back into the vineyard. "So, do you work on Sundays?"

"I do," he said. "Do you?"

She was tickled he'd asked. It meant he was sensitive to his employee's needs. "I do. Usually I work a few hours at the store in the morning and then teach a yoga class at night. But the spa is going to be closed tomorrow while Hunter finishes getting the new window in, so I'm free if you need me."

"Perfect. How about noon?" he asked, leading her to the golf cart that would take them back to the main house where her car was parked.

She climbed onto the cart, buckled in, and said, "I'm looking forward to it."

~

"HONEY, I'M HOME!" Shannon called as she walked into Hope's house.

"In here," Silas called back.

She followed the sound of his voice into the kitchen where she found her brother and Levi sitting at the table playing cards. Levi had his injured ankle propped up on a pillow on one of the chairs. "Where's the happy couple?"

"Date night," Levi said without looking up from his cards.

"Good for them." Shannon glanced at the kitchen, noting there were a pile of dishes in the sink, but it didn't look as if anyone had actually cooked anything. "Did you two have plans for dinner?"

Silas's head popped up. "Dinner? Are you making something?"

Shannon rolled her eyes. "Maybe."

"We can get pizza," Levi said. "Hope left some money on the counter."

She glanced over at the envelope off to the right and swallowed a groan. No way was she letting Hope and Chad buy dinner when she and Silas were invading them. "Is that what you want?"

Silas and Levi both shouted an enthusiastic, "Yes!"

"Pizza it is then." Shannon pulled her phone out of her pocket and made the call to the Mystyk Pizza Parlor. It was a newer place in town that had plenty of excellent choices.

Forty minutes later, Shannon was on her way back from picking up the pizza when she spotted a white van parked across the street from Hope's house. Unease coiled in her gut. Had that van been there before? She peered in the window as she drove by but couldn't see anything in the dusky twilight. Once she was out of her car and headed up the front walk, she glanced around for anyone suspicious. She didn't see anyone, but the hair on the back of her neck stood up, making her hurry into the house.

"Silas?" she called.

Her brother appeared in the living room, his phone pressed to his ear as he rolled his eyes and made a face to indicate how irritated he was. He mouthed, *Mom* and muttered something into the phone that sounded an awful lot like, "No effing way."

"What does she want?" Shannon hissed as she walked by with the pizza. They hadn't heard much from their mother since she'd informed them they were going to have to move out of her grandmother's house a few days ago. Shannon suspected that her mother was expecting them to call and beg her forgiveness or grovel to get the house back. Shannon would do neither.

"Same as always," Silas whispered. "Guilt trip."

"Of course." Shannon moved past him and brought the pizza to the table where Levi slumped in the chair, looking miserable. "Hey, Levi. What's wrong? Does your foot hurt?"

"Not really. I just iced it a few minutes ago."

Shannon grabbed some plates and silverware before taking a seat next to him. "Wanna talk about it?"

He glanced toward the living room, and worry flashed in his eyes before he dropped his gaze back to the cards still sitting in front of him. "What's there to talk about? Silas is going to go back home where he belongs, and I'll be here."

"Missing him," she finished for him.

Levi sighed. "Who wouldn't? I mean, he's Silas."

"He'll be back," she said, squeezing his hand. "He's already said he wants to spend the winter break here."

"Or in the Bahamas with his cast mates." He turned to Shannon. "He got an invite today."

Shannon chuckled. "What makes you think he'll go there when he can come up here and see us?"

"Come on, Shannon," Levi said, shaking his head. "Do you really think he's going to come to this small town when he can be drinking rum on the beach?"

"Yes, she does," Silas said, striding back into the dining room.

"Silas, I—"

"Nope. It's my turn to talk." Silas sat down next to Levi, leaning in close so that their shoulders brushed together.

Shannon got up and moved to the living room to give Levi and Silas some privacy. She felt for Levi. It never was easy being the one who was left behind. But she also knew Silas was serious about spending the holidays with her in Keating Hollow. He'd told her that very morning that, despite the turmoil with their mother and the paparazzi, he'd never felt quite so at peace as he did in the redwoods. He said it was good to spend time around people who really cared about him. She knew 'people' had meant her and Levi and that their acceptance of him, just for him and not his acting or fame or paycheck, was exactly what he needed most.

She moved to the window, eyeing the white van that was still parked across the street. A black SUV was parked behind it now, but she still didn't see any photographers. Was she being paranoid? Maybe. She pulled her phone out to call Brian, but before she could pull his number up, her phone started to ring.

Gigi. Great. Exactly who she didn't want to talk to. But she knew if she ignored the call, her mom would just keep trying. She was relentless when she wanted something.

"Shannon, it's about time you picked up your phone. I've been trying for ages to get you," her mom said without even uttering a hello.

"Good evening, Mother. How has your weekend been?" Shannon said.

"Don't be cute. I'm calling because I just got word of your stalker. It's time to come home, Shannon. You and Silas are not safe there in that little town. There's no protection from the crazy people who want a piece of Silas."

"Mom, I already told you Silas isn't interested in going home right now. He needs this break."

"I really don't care, Shannon. It isn't safe there for either of you. Just come home where we can keep the house gated and the insane internet trolls away from you and your brother. When things die down, you can go back to that little town of yours. I'm only saying this because I'm worried. I've seen the things they're saying about you online. Have you?"

"No. You know I don't look at that stuff." Shannon eyed the vehicles out front and started to feel uneasy all over again.

"You have to, darling. It's not good. Please just come home and let your father and I deal with this threat. Do you know what will happen if Silas is hurt?"

Shannon gritted her teeth together. And there is was. The real reason Gigi Ansell wanted her to pick up and run back to LA. Silas. She wanted him home, and she would do anything to get her way. But instead of arguing with her about it, she said, "I'll talk to Silas, and we'll get back to you."

"Shan—"

"Mom, I said we'll discuss it. That's the best I can do." Shannon ended the call and then turned off her phone before Gigi could blow it up when she tried to call back.

"She got to you, didn't she?" Silas said as he leaned against the wall closest to the kitchen.

Shannon ran a hand through his thick hair. "Kind of. As much as I don't want to go down there, she has a point. The house is gated. No one will be able to get to you."

Silas narrowed his eyes, and when he spoke again, there was a trace of venom in his tone. "Shannon, have you ever wondered who is really behind this circus we're living right now?"

"What does that mean? Drew said they arrested that gossip blogger and—"

Silas shook his head. "No. I mean who started this whole mess. Who told the press where we were? Who tipped them off to Brian's drama? Why are they still here when there's nothing to report? The paparazzi never sticks around this long unless there's a really juicy story or someone is paying them for their trouble."

"You mean like a bribe?" Shannon asked, her eyes raised in

surprise. "Who would do that?" Cara's people maybe. If she was trying to get publicity for her reality show, it made a certain amount of sense.

"People who are trying to get what they want, my dear sister. And what Mom wants most is to have not just me, but you too, home with her where she can control our lives. Think about it." He was angry now, practically vibrating with the emotion. "This is what she's best at, Shannon. Don't fall for her crap. Please."

Shannon didn't know what to say. Last night had been scary. If they had to endure something like that again, she really saw no choice but to do as her mother asked. She wouldn't risk Silas just because he was mad at their mother. Shannon was too, but with all the drama Gigi brought into their lives, the one thing she'd never done was put them in physical danger. She just couldn't believe her mother was behind the attack. "Mom wouldn't hire someone to throw a brick through the spa window," she said quietly.

Silas closed his eyes and let out a long sigh. When he opened them to look at her, he said, "You know, Shannon, a year ago I would've agreed with you. Now I'm not so sure. But there is one thing I agree with you about."

"What's that?"

He glanced back at the kitchen where he'd left Levi. "We can't stay here if there's more violence. I won't risk our friends getting hurt or their property being destroyed because of my fame."

Shannon wanted to argue, to insist it wasn't his fault. But she didn't because she was certain that he already knew that. It didn't change the fact that none of the paparazzi stuff would've happened if Silas hadn't come to town. "All right. Let's make a pact." She walked over to him and held her hand out. Silas took it and squeezed tightly. Shannon gave him a small grimace and continued, "If there is even a hint of more violence or property destruction, we'll head down to LA until things blow over. Together."

Silas groaned, but he nodded and shook her hand. Then he looked up at the ceiling and, as if he was praying to a higher power, said, "Please let the shenanigans of the past few days be over. We'd really like to enjoy the rest of the summer with our friends without anyone getting hurt."

"Amen," Shannon said.

Silas gave her a wry grin and disappeared back into the kitchen.

CHAPTER 23

*B*rian paced his living room for what felt like the hundredth time. As it turned out, no photographers were camped out in front of his place and hadn't been for at least the last twenty-four hours. He didn't know if they'd given up and gone back to LA or if they just weren't that interested in him. It was more than likely that pictures of him with Shannon were the money shots, and if they were watching her and Silas, they already knew Brian wasn't with them.

The thoughts didn't soothe him. It had been over two days since he'd spoken to Shannon, and he was starting to get worried. She had left him a message, but when he called her back, her voicemail had been full. He was minutes from jumping in his SUV and heading to town just to see if she was okay when his phone buzzed.

"Jacob, what's up?" he asked his friend.

"You tell me. What the hell happened at the Pelsh winery today?" Jacob asked.

Brian frowned. "What do you mean?

"Oh, hell. You don't know?"

"Obviously. Are they all right? What about Rex?" Brian asked.

"Turn on your television, channel 4. This is something you need to see to believe."

Brian walked over to his entertainment center and used the remote to find the right channel. As soon as the screen came into focus, the camera panned an aerial shot of the Pelshes' vineyard. There were rows and rows of grapes and... was that Shannon running through the vines? It was hard to tell because she was wearing a hat to shield her face from the sun and was carrying a red wand. Wasn't Shannon's wand sparkling turquoise? But it sure looked like her. No one else had red hair and curves like she did.

"Jacob, what the hell am I watching? Why is Shannon running through the vineyard?"

"Look at the vines on the edge of the property."

Brian scanned the screen and then muttered a curse when he saw bolts of fire being shot at the vines. One small section had been burned to a crisp. "Who the hell is doing that?"

"No one knows. It's a small group of people wearing all black. They just showed up and started screaming at Shannon, calling her a whore."

Brian's entire body went rigid. "They're calling her a whore? Because of me?"

"I think so, man." Jacob let out a long breath. "There's more."

"What?" he barked out, so angry he wanted to punch the wall. He refrained, however, knowing that would do nothing but potentially crack a few bones. He'd save the fists for someone who deserved it.

"Someone vandalized her grandmother's house. They

spray-painted *Brian and Cara 4Ever* on the door and then used fire magic to burn the same message into the lawn."

"Holy effing hell." Brian sank down on his couch, his head throbbing. "Who would do this? I'm no one in that world."

"But Cara is," Jacob said quietly. "You know that scene down there. Image is everything, and Cara's has taken a hit with the rumors you cheated and all."

"I didn't cheat on anyone!" Brian growled.

"I know, man. I just mean that's what the gossip rags have made everyone think," Jacob said. "You remember how it is. It's part of the reason we're here now."

Hadn't Brian been thinking the same thing only days before? "Yeah. I know. It's just... freakin' insane."

"No argument here," Jacob said. "Are you sure you're okay, man? Need me to come over? Head to the vineyard with you and check things out?"

"I'm fine. And no, but thanks," Brian said, not wanting Jacob to be pulled into this mess. He had Skye and Yvette to worry about. If people were burning the vineyard, who knew what else they'd do.

After Jacob ended the call, Brian sat back on his couch and tried Shannon one more time.

Voicemail full.

Dammit! He typed out a text message with just two words; *Call me.*

Then he waited and stared at the television.

The news anchor reported first on Silas and how he'd been in town visiting his sister while taking a break from the industry. There was speculation about a new reality show and whether or not he was going to return to his regular series in the fall. Then the story morphed into the gossip about Brian and Cara's engagement and Brian's alleged infidelity. They flashed a picture of Shannon leaving her house, but then it segued into one of Shannon and Rex standing in front of the Pelshes' home... kissing.

His eyes nearly bugged out of his head as he stared at the picture. Rex was kissing his girl? It wasn't possible, was it? Shannon wouldn't do that. Neither would Rex. But the proof was right there in front of his eyes. Rex had both hands on her cheeks, and his eyes were closed with his lips touching hers. Pictures didn't lie.

Something inside of Brian withered, and he felt the same way he had the day he found out he wasn't really Skye's father. He knew the situations weren't even remotely the same, but that didn't stop him from feeling as if his heart had been ripped clean out of his chest. He pressed a hand to his breastbone and did his best to stop the metaphoric bleeding.

He got up and went into his kitchen. Without any conscious thought, he pulled the whiskey bottle down and poured two fingers into a glass. Whiskey neat. It was what his father drank after a shit day. Brian let out a small bark of laughter. After all the time he'd spent trying to not be his father, it appeared the apple didn't fall too far from the tree.

As he sipped his whiskey, he remembered all the times he hadn't been mentally available for Sienna. How he'd always known he wasn't good for her. His presence in her life had only made things worse. And although Shannon was about as opposite a woman from Sienna as one could get, it appeared he wasn't good for her either. In the short time they'd been dating —bet or not—she'd been stalked by the paparazzi, had fake news stories written about her, and been cyber-stalked and terrorized by some insane individuals who didn't appear to be able to separate fiction from reality.

He glanced at the television where he'd frozen the picture

of Rex and Shannon. His friend was doing a damn fine job of taking care of his girl. Maybe it would be better if they *were* together. All Brian brought her was trouble. And that was the last thing he wanted for Shannon. She deserved the world, not a man who decided keeping his distance was best when things got hard.

Disgusted with himself, he turned the television off, poured the rest of his drink down the drain, and then changed into running gear, determined to run until the ache in his heart faded.

CHAPTER 24

"*I* can't believe I'm back here," Shannon said, gripping the wheel of the rental car so tightly her hands were starting to cramp. She stared at the closed gates of her parents' Hollywood Hills home and wondered if her credit card company would up her limit so that she could charge a hotel room instead. The debt would be worth it to not have to sleep under their roof.

Silas slumped down in his seat, and despite the fact it was eighty degrees outside, he was wearing a sweatshirt and had the hoody pulled so far down that his eyes were obscured. "Don't remind me. I was hoping this was all a nightmare and I'd wake up in Levi's room wondering why I was the one on the air mattress and not you."

"The answer is because I'm old and would be hunched over like a hag if I had to sleep on an air mattress," she said for the third time that week. The nights they'd stayed with Hope and Chad, Levi slept on the couch, while Shannon and Silas shared Levi's room. Shannon slept on his bed and Silas on an air mattress. It hadn't been ideal, but it was better than being stalked by crazy people.

"Right. You're so old," he said. "Better stock up on the Depends."

She felt a rumble of laughter rise up through her chest and was grateful for it. The day had been a pure nightmare. It started out normal enough. Shannon went to A Spoonful of Magic, boxed up some orders, did some administrative stuff, and then was at the Pelshes' winery by noon as promised. She and Rex spent the next hour working on tacking up some new vines, and just when they were ready for a break, a group of fire witches showed up and started torching a section of the vineyard. They kept chanting *whore, whore, whore* over and over again while Shannon and Rex made a run for it.

By the time Yvette and the other volunteer fire witches arrived, the group was already gone. Since they were wearing face paint, no one had recognized them, and there were no leads. To top it off, she later learned that her grandmother's house had been vandalized. Windows were broken and graffiti had been spray painted on the outside. That was the moment she knew she had to take Silas and get out of town. The irony was that he hadn't been targeted; *she* had. But she would not leave town without her little brother.

Silas hadn't been happy to leave Keating Hollow, or Levi for that matter. The two shared a long hug before Silas finally let go and scrambled into her car. Levi stood on the porch, leaning on his crutch, watching silently as they drove away. It was a bittersweet moment, and it made Shannon angry all over again that they were being forced to leave Keating Hollow.

The gates started to slide open, and Shannon groaned. They'd been idling in their spot for a few minutes, but Shannon hadn't yet found the nerve to press the intercom button. As it turned out, announcing their arrival wasn't necessary. "They've seen us."

"Mom probably had the maid watching the security cams to let her know the minute we arrived," Silas said.

Shannon glanced over at him. "Seriously? You have a full-time maid?"

He pushed the hoody back to look at her. "I find it disturbing that you're more surprised that Mom would have a maid at all rather than one she made stalk the security cameras."

Shannon cackled as she pulled forward into the Ansell compound. The property wasn't huge, but it was spacious enough, with a pretty flower garden in front of the house and a parking area in front of the garage that would easily fit up to five cars. In the rearview mirror, Shannon noted the gates closing. The anxiousness she'd been carrying with her in the pit of her stomach since the incident at the Pelshes' vineyard vanished. Breathing easier, she pulled the car into a spot that didn't block the driveway and killed the engine. She turned to Silas. "Ready?"

"Nope." But he climbed out of the car and was already retrieving their luggage by the time she joined him.

"Mr. Silas, please, I've got this," an older woman wearing a black and white maid uniform said as she rushed over. Her gray hair was pulled up into a severe bun, but her face was made up with flawless makeup that must've taken at least ten years off her age. "Your mother is anxiously waiting for you."

"Nah, Bett, I've got it. It's better for me if I flex my muscles every once in a while, anyway," he said, gently brushing her aside as he grabbed his and Shannon's suitcases.

"Hi, Bett," Shannon said, clutching her small carryon bag

and holding her hand out to the woman. "I'm Shannon, Gigi's daughter."

"Oh, Ms. Shannon. It's lovely to meet you." Bett pumped Shannon's hand while grabbing the carryon from her. "I'll carry this. Ms. Gigi won't like it if I let you both carry everything."

Shannon let go because she had no doubt that was true. "Thank you. That's very kind."

"Silas?" Gigi called the moment they walked through the door. "Is that you? I have news."

Silas rolled his eyes and whispered, "Of course she does."

Shannon glanced around at the house. It wasn't the same one they'd lived in while she was going to school at UCLA. It was bigger, in a nicer zip code, and had been decorated like something out of *Better Homes and Gardens*. There was white everywhere, with touches of turquoise and pale pink.

"This way." Silas jerked his head toward the sweeping staircase to the left and headed up to the second floor while Gigi continued to call for him from somewhere in the back of the house.

"Ms. Gigi is calling for you, Mr. Silas," Bett said.

"Tell her I'll be down in a few minutes, would you?" He gave her one of his dazzling smiles, and the maid blushed before she headed off to do his bidding.

"You have her wrapped around your finger," Shannon said.

"It's because I'm the only one who treats her like a person," he grumbled and dropped his suitcase in a room that was all black and white and mostly void of any personal possessions.

"Is that your room?" Shannon poked her head in. "It looks more like an upscale Airbnb situation."

He snorted. "That's what it feels like, too." Then he grinned and walked over to a door Shannon assumed was a closet. But when he opened it up, Shannon's eyes nearly bugged out at the fancy movie screen, oversized leather chairs, and mountain of video games in the corner. There was also a wet bar that was stocked with sodas, water, and juices, along with various snack items. "Holy cow. That's the nicest man cave I've ever seen."

"Yeah. It's not a bad place to hide out."

Shannon frowned. There still wasn't anything that was distinctly Silas about the space. There weren't any pictures of him and his friends, or family photos, or childhood mementos. Why was that?

He closed the door, led her out of his room and across the hall to another beautifully decorated guest room, and placed her suitcase inside the door. "Drop your stuff here, and after we greet the parentals, let's meet in my man cave. We can watch a movie and pretend we never left Keating Hollow."

Shannon dropped her purse in the corner and said, "Works for me."

After washing up, Shannon followed Silas downstairs and down a hallway that led to an oversized office where their mother sat behind a large banker's desk.

"Silas. Finally," she said, standing and coming around to wrap him in her embrace. "I missed you, darling."

Her brother patted their mother's back but didn't respond.

Gigi, who was dressed in a white linen pantsuit and peach colored silk shirt, pulled back and scanned him, tsking and shaking her head as she muttered, "Gonna need to get the stylist in here first thing in the morning. Your hair needs highlights, brows need waxing, and we probably need a facial and a manicure. We need you looking your best for those meetings tomorrow afternoon."

A muscle pulsed in Silas's jaw. "What meetings?"

Shannon leaned against the doorframe of her mother's

office and wondered if the woman had even noticed her standing there.

Gigi let Silas go and returned to her desk chair, kicking back with her fingers laced behind her head. "With the network execs. If we're going to get this project off the ground, we need to move it."

Silas stared at her for a long moment. Then he shook his head and walked out of the room.

"Silas! Cut it out, already. I've had just about enough of your surly attitude!" she shouted after him, her lips twisting into a scowl. When he still didn't answer, she turned her attention to the paperwork cluttering her desk.

Shannon watched her through narrowed eyes, and when the woman still didn't acknowledge her presence, Shannon walked all the way in and closed the door behind her.

"I don't want to hear it, Shannon," Gigi said without looking up from what appeared to be an old-school appointment book.

"Oh, so you did notice I'm here," Shannon said, taking a seat in a chair across the desk from her mother.

"Of course I did. You've been glaring at me this whole time. I'm not in the mood to argue with you, too. I shouldn't need to explain that I'm doing everything in my power to *help* Silas, not annoy him."

"It's probably not helping him if your plans for his career make him want to leave Hollywood for good," Shannon said calmly.

Her head snapped up. "He's not you. There's no way he's quitting the business."

"Maybe not," Shannon said. "But he will leave you as soon as he gets the chance if you keep this up."

Gigi rolled her eyes. "Why would he leave me? I've made him a very rich young man."

"You mean he's made himself a very rich young man," Shannon corrected. "You just opened the doors for him."

"I did more than just open doors," Gigi hissed, her ire in full swing now as she stood and placed her palms flat on her desk. "You have no idea what I've had to do to find opportunities for that boy. And if he thinks he's going to leave me for one of the other sharks in this town, then he needs to grow up. No one cares about him more than I do."

"Really, Mom? I think you might be mistaken." Shannon rose and moved toward the door.

"What are you talking about?" Gigi demanded.

Shannon shook her head and walked out. There was no reason to put a target on her own back this soon. If her mother knew Silas had already asked Shannon to be his manager once he was eighteen, she'd do everything in her power to undermine that decision for the next eight months. Shannon probably shouldn't have said anything at all, but watching her mother try to walk all over Silas had put her in protective mode. She wanted nothing more than for her and Silas to get back on that plane for Keating Hollow and never look back. But they couldn't, and they both knew it.

"Hey! There's my girl," a familiar male voice boomed from the kitchen as she walked by. "Come here and give your old man a hug."

Shannon felt a smile tug at her lips, and she moved into her dad's arms. "Dad! I didn't even know you were home."

"Just got back from a business meeting down in San Diego," Nate Ansell said, hugging her tightly. "Looks like your old dad is going to invest in a microbrewery."

"Really?" Still holding on to him, she glanced up into his

kind face. "I had no idea you knew anything about microbreweries."

"I don't." He chuckled. "But my business partners do. My job is to bring the investors." He winked at her. "That means I plunk down cash and get my poker buddies to do the same."

Shannon stepped back and laughed. "Well, as long as you're happy and having fun, that's all that matters, I guess."

"That's what I keep telling your mother." He glanced around. "Did you bring your brother home with you?"

She nodded. "He's upstairs fuming about some meetings he doesn't want to take."

"Did your mother already line those up?" His expression was stormy as he started to move toward the hallway.

"It appears so."

He glanced back at her. "I told her to let you kids get your feet under you before she started in on that damned reality show again. After everything you went through..." He shook his head. "She's more and more like a machine every day. Tell Silas not to worry about this. I'll handle it." He stalked down the hallway and a moment later, she heard her mother's office door slam closed.

Shannon gaped after her father. Was this the same man she'd grown up with? He'd always let their mom call the shots and deferred to her on the management side of things. She was the force behind making their business successful, so he left her to it. It appeared times had changed. Finally, and for the better. He'd always had a good heart. Maybe he had finally opened up his eyes to see what damage Gigi was causing. She loved him for standing up for Silas.

When Shannon got back upstairs, she took a moment to try to call Brian again. Now that her mother and the press had stopped blowing her phone up every five minutes, she'd turned it back on and cleared out her voicemail. She'd found one text from Brian asking her to call him, and guilt had consumed her. She should have called him right after the incident at the Pelshes' vineyard, but she'd been too busy making arrangements to leave town, including contacting Miss Maple, Rex, and Faith to let them all know she wouldn't be coming to work for a week or so. By the time she and Silas were on their way to the airport, she'd passed out and fallen into a fitful sleep.

It had been one hell of a day.

Brian's phone went straight to voicemail. She left him a message, letting him know where she was and why but that she'd be back for Faith and Hunter's wedding, even if she came in for just the day. She wasn't going to miss it for the world.

"Silas?" she called as she knocked on his bedroom door.

The door was flung open, and her brother strode back into his room, which looked like it had exploded. Clothes were everywhere, along with a pile of pictures and a few old stuffed animals she hadn't seen since he was a little boy.

"What's going on?" she asked hesitantly, wondering where he'd been keeping his childhood mementos. Under the bed?

"I'm getting out of here. She's insane." He hauled a second large suitcase out of his closet and started throwing random clothes inside.

"Okay. I agree. She's nutso. But where are you going to go?"

He stopped suddenly and stared up at the ceiling as he ran both hands through his hair. "I have no idea, Shan. Just... anywhere but here."

Tears stung the backs of her eyes as she watched her sweet brother have a complete meltdown. But she blinked them back and did what her mother should have been doing. She walked over to him and gave him a big hug. "It will get better, Si. I promise."

"I don't want this anymore. I can't take it." He pressed his face against her shoulder and held on.

"I know." She ran her hand down his back, trying to comfort him. After a moment, she said, "I think Dad might be putting his foot down with her right now. When he learned she'd set up those meetings without your consent, he sort of lost it."

Silas pulled out of her embrace and shoved his hands in his jean pockets. "What do you mean?"

"He strode in there, all angry, and slammed the door." Shannon sat down on his bed. "I don't know what will come of it, but I've never known him to do that before."

Silas sat next to her, his brows drawn together in confusion. "That's strange. He never questions her."

Muffled footsteps sounded in the hall outside Silas's door just before their father appeared. He walked in, his faced pinched in irritation, but when he saw his children, his expression softened. "It's so good to see you two together."

Shannon moved over, leaving room between her and Silas, and patted the bed. "Come take a seat."

He smiled and sat between them, draping his arms over their shoulders and pulling them in for sideways hugs. "I've missed you both."

"I haven't been gone that long, Dad," Silas said.

"Physically no, but mentally yes," he said. "You've been withdrawn for a while now."

Silas sighed. "Yeah, maybe."

"He's too stressed, Dad. Mom has—" Shannon started.

"Your mother and I had a talk just now, and we've come to an agreement," Nate Ansell said.

"And what's that?" Silas asked, not bothering to hide his skepticism.

"There will be no business talk for the next week. Since Shannon is here, we're going to just be a family. No meetings, no negotiations, nothing business related unless it's a true emergency."

Silas scoffed. "No way, Dad. You know that's never going to work. She'll have producers and directors stopping by 'unexpectedly' for 'social' calls by tomorrow afternoon."

"Well, if she does, the three of us will get into the car and hit Disneyland or something. She can deal with them."

Shannon let out a bark of laughter. "You know what, old man?"

"What?" he asked, turning to her with amusement dancing in his eyes. Eyes that were so much like her own.

"You're all right." Shannon leaned in and kissed him on the cheek, suddenly feeling okay with the fact that she'd come home.

CHAPTER 25

$\mathcal{B}$rian sat in his SUV in front of the house Shannon had lived in up until a few days ago, lamenting the senseless vandalism he saw there and listening to her voicemail message for the fifth time. She'd called the night before to let him know she was in LA for the foreseeable future, but he hadn't called her back. He couldn't. Not now. Not after seeing her kissing Rex, not to mention the fact that he'd caused her far too many problems recently. What he needed to do was give them both some space for a while. And calling her, hearing her voice, would only make him want to get on a plane and head to LA as soon as possible to find out who she really wanted, him or Rex. But the media storm that would follow made him shudder in revulsion.

No. If there was any chance his presence in her life would put her or her brother in danger or cause her pain, he couldn't justify seeing her. He needed to keep his distance for now. And keeping in touch via phone calls would only make that harder. With his heart hammering against his ribcage, he tapped out a message to Shannon that said he was going on a business trip overseas and would be away for at least a few days. After he hit *Send*, he felt an odd sense of loss and sadness wash over him as if he'd just let her go for good.

His phone buzzed with a message immediately, and although he told himself it was better to ignore it, he opened up the text from Shannon and smiled when he saw the picture of her blowing him a kiss. The caption read, *Travel safe. Can't wait to see you at Faith's wedding.*

He groaned. Should he still show up for that date? He had no idea. The only thing he did know was that it was time to make sure the paparazzi stopped bothering her, and if he had to play hardball, then that's what he'd do.

He tapped his father's name in his contacts list, and when William Knox answered, Brian said, "Dad? I need your help."

"Shoot," his father said.

"Do you know anyone who can plant a story? I'm no longer willing to wait for Cara to do the right thing," Brian said.

His dad let out a low laugh. "Actually, I know just the guy."

When Brian ended the call five minutes later, he felt lighter than he had in days. He jumped out of his SUV, grabbed the paint supplies he'd brought, and went to work covering up the vandalism on the cottage Shannon had called home for so long.

THREE DAYS HAD GONE by since Shannon and Silas had arrived in LA. And after their dad had a chat with their mom, something magical had happened; Gigi Ansell hadn't said a word about the show she wanted Silas to do.

Shannon was cautiously happy, while Silas was waiting for the other shoe to drop. He had trouble believing that she'd put the idea on the backburner just because Nate asked her to.

"I've been around this block too many times," Silas told Shannon as he drove them to a beach party hosted by one of his costars. "She behaves for an unspecified amount of time, and then she drops a bomb on you. I'm just waiting for the fallout."

"That's pretty cynical for a seventeen-year-old," she said, feeling slightly ridiculous for tagging along with her little brother, but Silas had insisted there'd be guests of all ages.

"Show business will do that to a guy," he said.

"I know." Her phone buzzed with an incoming message. Shannon glanced at it and groaned.

"What now?"

"Mom sent me an article about Brian and Cara." She considered just deleting the text. Did she really want to read the latest gossip? She believed Brian when he said there wasn't anything going on there. She didn't need to read anything else.

But then another text from her mother arrived. *Looks like you found a trustworthy one this time.*

Shannon couldn't ignore that. She hit the link and read the headline to Silas. "Cara Manchester and Brian Knox were never engaged."

"Finally," he said. "Is it a reputable source?"

"Yes. It's *Cali Style,* the same one that broke the original story," Shannon confirmed.

"Good. That should be the end of that." He grinned at her. "Congrats, sis, you survived your first Hollywood scandal."

"Thank the gods for small favors," she said, scanning the new report. The article went on to state it was all a publicity stunt by Cara Manchester, according to inside sources at Newport Broadcasting, the station that was producing the reality show Cara was starring in that fall. After she was done reading, she sent her mother a short text thanking her. It was no surprise to Shannon when her mother didn't respond.

Silas pulled into a long driveway and parked the Porsche they'd had delivered from Keating Hollow the day before next to a sleek silver Tesla.

Shannon eyed the dozen or so high-end cars and let out a whistle. "We're not in Keating Hollow anymore, Toto."

Silas let out a sigh. "Nope. Too bad, too, because I'd much rather be there than here right now." He shoved his hands into his front pockets and led the way up the flower-lined walkway to the front door.

"Same. But we can suffer here for a bit, right?" Shannon said with a quick wink.

"I guess." He shook hands with the young man who opened the door and introduced her to his costar.

The young man invited them in, and as soon as Shannon rounded the corner to the main living room, she let out an audible gasp. The entire back wall was made of glass, and the ocean view was incredible. All she could see was the beautiful water of the Pacific and miles of beach. Man, she could get used to that view... but only if it was right next to Keating Hollow. As mesmerizing as the ocean was, it was no substitute for the small community of people she had waiting for her back home.

"Here." Silas pressed a drink into her hand and tugged her outside onto the patio. There was a slight breeze that made the day heavenly.

"Mind if I just hang out here in the sunshine?" she asked him.

"Of course not. Why are you even asking?" He took a long swig of his drink out of the red Solo cup.

"Because I'm about to be hugely antisocial as I sit out here and soak up the rays." She eyed the contents of his cup. "What are you drinking?"

"Ginger beer," he said and shoved it under her nose.

Because he was a teenager at an industry party, instead of just smelling it, she took a sip. Sure enough, ginger beer. "All right. Go mingle. Don't let anyone spike your drink."

He rolled his eyes, "Yes, Mom." But as he walked back into the house, she didn't miss his lips twitching with amusement.

"That's right, little bro. No partying while I'm around," she called after him.

He lifted his right hand and gave her the finger.

Snickering, she settled herself onto one of the lounge chairs and promptly dozed off. Shannon woke with a start, unsure of what it was that startled her awake. She lay on the chair, unmoving, as she listened to the waves crashing on the mostly deserted beach and admired the late afternoon sunlight bouncing off the blue waters.

"I heard he was leaving the biz for good," a woman said, her voice carrying on the breeze.

Shannon glanced around, looking for the woman, and finally spotted a model-tall blonde on the other side of the patio with a shorter, dark-haired woman. They were both holding wine glasses and had their heads bent together as if they were speaking in confidence. They had their backs to her, and Shannon guessed that because of where she was positioned they hadn't even noticed her when they stepped outside.

"Doesn't look like it. He's here today, isn't he?" the shorter one said.

"But for how long? The first time I ever met Silas, the first thing he did was warn me about reading the gossip rags. He said none of it is true, and often all it does is hurt the actor. He was pretty vehement about it, too. If he ever finds out what his mother has been doing to manipulate his career, I bet he'll quit and never come back. Can you imagine? Your mom is supposed to be protecting you, not making your life miserable."

Shannon stiffened at the first mention of Silas's name. But when the woman said their mom was manipulating him, her entire body went rigid. What exactly did she mean? What did she know?

The brunette shook her head in disgust. "My ex, Randy Randolf, you remember him, right? He works for *Total Gossip*. Anyway, he told me that Gigi herself was calling in tips about where Silas was when he just disappeared from LA. And she fed them the story about Cara Manchester that had a direct effect on Silas's sister. I swear that woman is the worst publicity whore."

Shannon's chest got tight, and suddenly she was having trouble breathing. Were these women right? Had Gigi been pulling the publicity strings the entire time? It made sense. She wanted Silas to come home. What better way than to make his stay in Keating Hollow miserable? But why had she fed them Cara's story? Just to fuel the flames?

"Randy told you that?" the blonde asked. "Why?"

"Pillow talk. You know how it is. Sex with the ex happens, and Randy always gets chatty afterward."

They laughed and continued to talk about post-breakup sex, and then after a few moments, they disappeared back inside. Shannon sat up, rubbed at her eyes, and then typed the name *Randy Randolf* into her phone. Sure enough, his name popped up as a reporter with *Total Gossip*.

Shannon stared at her phone and tried to swallow the pure

disgust that rose from the depths of her gut. Their own mother sent the gossip rags after them. Property had been destroyed. People could've been hurt. And it was all because Gigi Ansell hadn't gotten what she wanted. She sent Silas a text. *We need to go. Meet me at the car.*

CHAPTER 26

"*I* knew it!" Silas raged as they strode into their parents' house.

Shannon decided to wait to tell him what she'd heard until they got home. She knew he'd be furious, and who could blame him?

"Remember when I said she was probably behind the gossip? Son of a... she has no moral compass. I can't do this shit anymore." He ran up the stairs, presumably to pack again.

Shannon watched him go and then calmly walked back to her mother's office. The door was cracked open slightly, and Shannon could hear her talking on the phone to one of her many contacts. She backed away and went in search of her father. She found him sitting in a chair in the sunroom at the back of the house, reading on his e-reader.

"Hey, Shan," he smiled at her, his eyes lighting up as if he was genuinely pleased to see her. "How was the beach? You look like you got a little sun."

"It was gorgeous. I can't imagine what it must be like to live right on the beach like that year-round," she said.

"Expensive." He chuckled and put his e-reader down. "Something's on your mind, isn't it?"

Shannon perched on the wicker couch next to him. "Can I ask you something about Grandma's house?"

"Sure, sweet pea. Does it need some upgrades? I'm not sure how much life that roof has in it."

"Um..." She frowned. "I'm not sure. There haven't been any problems with the roof if that's what you mean. It could use a paint job now that it's been vandalized, but—"

"Vandalized?" He sat up straight and peered at her with concerned eyes. "Since when? What happened? I thought Keating Hollow was a safe town. It was when we lived there. Vandalism was never an issue. Do we need to think about selling?"

Shannon blinked at him, momentarily stunned that he was so clueless about what had happened in Keating Hollow. Then she took a deep breath and told him everything. "Dad, Mom kicked me out. She said it's time to sell the place. But the day we came down here, someone spray painted the words *Brian and Cara 4Ever* all over Grandma's house. So if you're going to sell, it needs—"

"I never said we were going to sell that house." He rose to his feet and started moving toward the hallway. "She has no right to make a decision like that." He paused and glanced back at Shannon. "Let's go. We need to clear a few things up with your mother."

His tone was commanding, and Shannon didn't think twice. She followed him into her mother's office and then was completely quiet for over an hour as she watched her parents fight about the house, her dad's intention to sign it over to Shannon, and then how he managed to get her mother to confess everything she'd been up to regarding Silas's career over the last month.

Eventually, Shannon chimed in with, "Don't forget to tell him about Randy Randolf."

Gigi went completely white at the mention of the gossip reporter's name. "How... um, how did you know about that?"

"Nobody can keep a secret in this town, Mother. You know that better than anyone," Shannon said, unwilling to reveal her sources.

"Gigi, what did you do?" Nate demanded.

Shannon leaned against the wall of the office and waited.

Gigi hung her head and muttered a curse.

"Out with it," Shannon's father said, sounding like his temper might explode at any moment.

"I just wanted Silas to come home," she said. "That deal... it won't just help him. Our new client, Jordon James, stands to get a reality show too if we can make this happen. It's good for all of us, Nate. I didn't know those internet stalkers would show up and threaten Shannon. That wasn't my intention. I would never—"

"It doesn't matter what your intention was, Mom," Shannon said, cutting her off. "It happened, and it happened because you were selfish. And even after you found out, you didn't do anything about it, did you?"

"I did," she said, her voice trembling now. "I called in a favor and had that GNT blog shut down, Shannon. I swear it. I'm sorry. That is not what I wanted. Of course it wasn't. You're my children. Do you really think I wanted something bad to happen to you?"

"You did kick them out of my mother's house," Nate said.

Gigi's face turned another shade of white as she turned to her husband.

"And you told Shannon you were going to sell that house, didn't you?"

"Yes, but—"

"It's not yours to sell, Gigi." Nate walked over to the filing cabinet in the corner of her office. After riffling through one of the drawers, he pulled out a manila envelope and handed it to Shannon.

"What's this?" she asked him.

"The deed to my mother's house." He smiled gently. "I always intended to give it to you as a wedding present, but that seems pretty archaic now that I think about it, doesn't it? The paperwork is all there. All you have to do is file it and the house is yours, sweet pea."

Gigi sniffled and wiped at her eyes.

Nate turned to her. "You and I will discuss this insanity more later. Right now, I'm going to go talk to our son and find out what he wants after this fiasco. Goodness, Gigi. What were you thinking?"

"I wanted him to have a successful career. He wasn't listening to me and—"

"He already has a successful career," Shannon said. "I can tell you what he wants. He asked me to be his manager when he turns eighteen."

"But you don't even live down here!" Gigi exclaimed.

"That's what I said. He doesn't care. All he wants is someone who is one hundred percent on his side without an agenda of their own," Shannon explained.

"I can do that," Gigi said, using a handkerchief to dab at her eyes.

"No, Gigi," Nate said, shaking his head. "You will always try to grab at things beyond everyone's reach. I think it's time to let Silas go." He turned to Shannon. "Tell Silas I'll be up to talk to him in a bit. I'll bring the new representation paperwork, and by this evening, *you'll* be his new manager."

Shannon stared in wonder at her father. She'd never seen him take charge before. Not like this. Gigi was a whimpering mess, and it was clear she wouldn't argue with him. It made her wonder what kind of marriage they really had when no one was watching. Of course she'd been gone for a decade. It wasn't unreasonable to think that the dynamics of their relationship had changed.

"Go, Shannon. Your mother and I need to talk," he urged.

"Thanks, Dad." She pulled him into a quick hug and ran upstairs to tell her brother the good news.

"I'm getting the hell out of here," Silas all but snarled when Shannon walked into his bedroom.

She grinned and pulled him into a tight hug.

Silas let out a grunt of surprise, but he hugged her back and asked, "What's going on, Shan?"

When she pulled back, she pressed both palms to his cheeks and said, "We're going home. Home to Keating Hollow. And thanks to Dad, I'm your new manager, effective immediately."

"What?" He stepped back and shook his head. "Did you just say what I think you said?"

She nodded, happy tears stinging her eyes. "Yes, baby bro. Go ahead and text Levi, cause we're leaving first thing in the morning."

"You don't think the paparazzi is still going to be stalking us there?" he asked.

"Have they been here once?" she countered.

He shook his head and scowled. "Right. That was Mom's doing. What makes you think she won't try that again?"

Shannon smirked. "Because you're no longer her client. You're mine. And Dad now knows everything she did. So don't worry about a thing. We're out of here, and you don't need to come back until filming begins for *Timekeeper*."

Silas sat down on his bed, a range of emotions flashing through his eyes. Apprehension, disbelief, and then pure joy lit his gaze and he threw back his head and let out a laugh. "I can't believe it. Keating Hollow for the next month? You're serious?"

Shannon pulled out her phone and tapped one of her apps. "I'm dead serious. I'm booking our flights right now. Be ready before the crack of dawn.

CHAPTER 27

"*S*hannon!" Hope cried as she threw her door open. "You're home!" She glanced around her friend and smiled at Silas. "Hey Silas. We're all excited you're going to spend the rest of the summer here. There's someone in the kitchen who's dying to see you."

Shannon moved aside to let Silas slip into the house.

He waved at Hope and rushed in, making a beeline for the back of the house.

"Si!" they heard Levi exclaim, followed by the two boys laughing.

"I'm glad someone is having a nice reunion," Shannon said as she stepped back and sat in the porch swing.

Hope followed her. "You mean your reunion with Brian didn't go so well?"

"What reunion? He's not even in town, and he's not returning my texts." Shannon's homecoming had turned sour when she hadn't been able to get in touch with Brian. He'd sent a text several days earlier letting her know he was going out of town for a few days, but he hadn't said specifically where. She was dying to see him, to let him know they were all clear and didn't need to keep taking the break he'd insisted on.

She and Silas had been home for a day and a half, and so far there hadn't been a lick of trouble. After their plane had landed, they'd spent the rest of the day moving all of Shannon's stuff back into her grandmother's house—soon to be her house. The one that had been freshly painted and the broken windows replaced, though none of her neighbors seemed to have a clue who'd taken care of that job. Shannon would've suspected Brian, but he'd been out of town.

"What gave you that idea?" Hope asked. "He's in town. He came in for a massage this morning. That shoulder of his really tightened up after all that painting he did."

"Painting?" Shannon narrowed her eyes at her friend. "Are you saying he's the one who fixed up my grandmother's house?"

Hope leaned forward and gave her a puzzled look. "You mean you didn't know?"

Shannon shook her head slowly. "He told me he had to go overseas for a bit and would be out of touch. I haven't heard from him since." But that didn't make sense. If he'd painted her house and was in town, why hadn't he returned her call or her text she's sent letting him know she was headed home?

"Oh, honey." Hope patted Shannon's knee. "It sounds like the two of you need to talk."

"No kidding. But if he isn't returning my calls..." Frustration bubbled up and spilled over into a huff of irritation. "I don't get it."

"Of course you don't," Hope said, laughing. "He's a man. You're not supposed to." She stood and held out her hand to help her friend out of the swing. "Tell you what... Why don't you hop in that car of yours and head up to Brian's beautiful house on the hill? Silas can stay here with us tonight. I'm sure he and Levi are going to want to play video games and eat junk food all night anyway. You go and find out what's going on in Brian's thick head and let me worry about the rest."

Shannon didn't hesitate. She pulled Hope into a quick hug, thanked her for being the best friend a girl could have, and then rushed to her car. It wasn't until she was halfway down Main Street that she realized she didn't even have Brian's address. After a quick stop at Yvette's bookstore to ask her for directions, she was back in her car and on her way up the mountain.

BRIAN READ Shannon's text for what seemed like the hundredth time. She was home, back at her grandmother's cottage. And he was sitting in his house, acting as if that didn't mean something to him. All he could ask himself was *what the hell is wrong with me?*

He knew the answer. But that didn't mean he wanted to face the fact that he wasn't any good for her. He hadn't been able to protect her when crazy stalkers came for her. He'd even been the reason they'd harassed her. It was just like the fact he hadn't been good for Sienna. She'd gotten sick, and he'd only made it worse by enabling her destructive behavior. If only he'd insisted on her seeing a psychologist sooner, things might not have gotten so bad. He was tired of being the man that caused issues for the women in his life; he wanted to be the one who made things better.

The phone grew warm in Brian's hand. He moved his finger to delete Shannon's latest message but found he couldn't do it. It was too much like deleting her from his life. And as much as he was determined to leave her alone now, he couldn't erase any of the traces of her. It was too painful.

Groaning, he dropped his phone onto the counter and headed for his kitchen. After tying on an apron, he pulled out his favorite stainless steel mixing bowl, flour, sugar, and butter, intending to make shortbread cookies. He wasn't hungry. He hadn't been since right about the time Shannon left town. But he needed to do something to keep his hands busy, or he'd—

The doorbell rang, followed by loud knocking on the door.

He dropped the stick of butter he'd been holding onto the granite countertop and went to find out who'd gone through the trouble to drive halfway up the mountain to see him in person. Brian wiped his hands on his apron and opened the door. "Shannon?"

She walked right in without even saying a word.

"Hey," he said, joy warming him from the inside out like a ray of sunshine. Gods, he'd missed her even more than he'd realized.

She spun around and placed her hands on her hips and said, "Care to explain why you lied to me about going out of town?"

"Only if you care to explain to me why you were kissing Rex." The words were out of his mouth before he could stop them. He hadn't had any intention of confronting her with what he saw on that news program, but there it was. He wasn't even sure he wanted the answer, but it was too late now.

"What?" Her face scrunched up in confusion. "I wasn't kissing Rex. What makes you think that? I haven't even seen him or talked to him since the day the vineyard was vandalized by those fire witches."

"I saw it on the newscast, Shannon. He was cupping your face with both hands, and his lips were on yours." He was pissed now. It was one thing to kiss one of his best friends. It was entirely another to act as if it hadn't happened.

The crease in her forehead only deepened. "Rex did not kiss me," she insisted. "He did cup my cheeks, but that's because I was freaking out and he was trying to calm me down. But he definitely didn't kiss me. Why would he do that? He's your friend."

She seemed so adamant, so sure. Had his eyes been deceiving him? He didn't think so. He knew what he'd seen. Brian walked up to her, placed both hands on her cheeks and then bent his head so that his lips were just barely brushing hers. "Are you telling me this isn't the exact scene I saw on my television?"

She lifted her gaze to his and, in a firm voice, said, "That's exactly what I'm saying." She knocked his hands away, placed hers on his cheeks, and brought her face really close to his as she looked him in the eye. "Rex was trying to calm me down. He did it by making me focus on him just like this. When he was done talking to me, he pressed a kiss to my forehead and then put me in my car. Just like this." She pressed up onto her tiptoes and brushed a soft kiss over his skin.

His entire body started to tingle with desire from that slight kiss, and he let out a barely audible groan.

Shannon stepped back, taking her soft hands with her. "Is that why you've been avoiding me? Because you thought I had a thing with Rex?"

"Yes." He grimaced and added, "No. Not really."

"Then why?" she demanded.

"Because, Shannon." He threw his hands up. "Do you think any of this would've happened to you if it weren't for me? If you hadn't been dragged into the drama with Cara, no one would've come for you. You wouldn't have been hurt, Faith's spa wouldn't have had a brick thrown through the window, and the Pelshes' vineyard never would've been burned. I didn't handle the problem with Cara very well. Not until it was too late, anyway. I... It seemed better for you if I kept my distance."

Shannon was speechless. Was he kidding? "You can't be serious."

"I'm dead serious. First I didn't handle things with Sienna well. Then I didn't take the Cara situation seriously enough, and you almost got hurt because of me."

Shannon shook her head and stepped close to him again, pressing her palms to his chest. "Brian, shut up."

"What?" He couldn't help but chuckle. Her response was so perfectly her.

"My mom was the reason the paparazzi was even here. If we want to blame anyone, it's her. Not you. And before you go blaming yourself again, please try to remember you can't be responsible for other people's actions. Especially crazy people."

"I didn't want to bring you any more drama," he said, sliding his arms around her waist, suddenly unable to keep from touching her.

"Silas and I brought plenty of our own. Can we drop this and move on? I'm feeling the need to settle up on that bet we made."

"I'm more than happy to move on." He dipped his head and ran his lips along her jawline before pressing a soft kiss to her lips. "But what do you mean settle up on that bet? By my last count, we still have four dates to cover."

"I'm surrendering. I already know I'm going to lose, so how about we take care of the naked massage portion right now? Because I can't wait to get my hands on you."

"Holy hell, Shannon," Brian whispered as he started

maneuvering her through his house toward the bedroom. "You do realize I'll never be able to keep my hands to myself, right?"

"That's what I was counting on." The moment they were in his bedroom, Shannon turned him so that his back was pressed up against the wall. She removed his apron and ran her hands under his T-shirt, reveling in his well-defined chest. Then she slipped one hand down to cup his perfect butt while she kissed him with everything she had. When she finally broke away, Brian was breathing heavily, and his dark eyes were swimming with pure desire. She once again moved in close, pressed both of her palms to his cheeks, and when his breath caught, she said, "Get naked."

CHAPTER 28

*S*hannon stood behind the counter at A Spoonful of Magic and tried to suppress her yawn. After her marathon completely naked massage session with Brian had turned into an all-night love fest, she'd ended up getting only a couple hours of sleep before heading into work. She'd didn't mind though. Her time in Brian's bed had been worth every delicious second.

"Stop smiling like you won the lottery. It's making me cranky," Miranda Moon said from her usual spot at one of the shop's tables. She was a paranormal romance author who'd moved to town over the summer and had claimed one of A Spoonful of Magic's tables as one of her favorite spots to work. "You look like you've been thoroughly… erm, satisfied."

Shannon laughed. "I don't kiss and tell."

"There's no reason to. It's written all over you," she said.

"Sorry?" Shannon picked up her wand and aimed it at Miranda's empty dishes. They floated effortlessly past Shannon and right into the sink where they were rinsed and then placed into the dishwasher without Shannon having to lift a finger.

"Nice trick," Miranda said. "I think I'm going to put it in this book. Any tips on how to get it right?"

Shannon held up her gorgeous whore-red wand. "You need a good connection with your wand, and the secret is in the wrist. This one is swish and flick and point." Shannon demonstrated on the dirty napkin in front of Miranda. "Like this." She aimed the wand and showed her the motions, and they both watched as the napkin floated through the air and landed in the nearby trash can.

"Awesome. I just have to hope it doesn't go haywire, too."

"What do you mean?" Shannon asked.

Miranda waved a hand, indicating it wasn't important.

But Shannon was insistent. "Are you having trouble with your magic?"

"No not really. I just... I've never had trouble getting a date before. You know what I mean?" She stood up and twirled around, showing off her curvy figure that was laced up in a black corset dress. "This usually does all the work, you know?"

Shannon chuckled as she eyed the woman's cleavage peeking out from the top of the dress. "I can imagine. That style really works for you."

"Right?" Miranda glanced down at herself and sighed. "I'm starting to think I'm losing my touch, and it's making me slightly crazy."

The bells on the door chimed, and Rex Holiday strode in. A big smile broke out on his face when he spotted Shannon. "Hey there, stranger. It's good to see you back in town."

"Hi, Rex. It's better than good to be back. How's the vineyard?"

"It's better," he said. "Abby came by, and together we were able to salvage most of the damaged vines."

"That's good news." Shannon helped him pick out a present for Abby Townsend as a thank you for her help, and while Shannon was wrapping it up, Miranda Moon made her way to the counter and brushed her arm up against Rex's.

"Hey there, handsome." She glanced up at him, all innocence, with her big dark eyes.

Rex smiled down at her, obvious interest flashing over his features as he scanned her from head to toe. *Miranda was right,* Shannon thought. That dress was a secret weapon.

But then just as Shannon tried to hand the package to Rex, Miranda reached out, accidentally knocking it to the ground.

"Oh, no. I'm so sorry." She bent down to retrieve the package at the same time that Rex did, but as she grabbed for the package, she completely missed and instead grabbed an entirely different package.

Rex's package.

Rex let out a yelp and scrambled back, pressing one hand against his crotch and clutching the package with the other.

Miranda's face flushed bright red, and she stammered her apologies as Rex hurried out of the shop. "Oh. Em. Gee," Miranda said as she slumped into her chair. "I can't believe that just happened."

Shannon couldn't help the laughter that rumbled up from her chest. "Holy hell, Miranda. I see what you mean. That dress was doing its job, and then everything went to crap in ten seconds flat."

Miranda pressed the back of her hand to her forehead. "I think I'm cursed. That's the only explanation."

"Or just klutzy," Shannon teased. But she wondered if Miranda really was cursed. Not long ago, Miss Maple had neutralized a crude love spell that had been attached to Miranda's preferred table.

"Maybe. I'm going to go home and drown my embarrassment in a bottle of wine. See you at the wedding Friday night?"

"Definitely. Brian and I will be there with bells on." Shannon pulled a couple of chocolates out of the case and walked them over to Miranda. "Here. To go with the wine."

Miranda gave her a grateful smile.

"Listen," Shannon said, making an effort to expand her social circle. "I'm having a small pool party on Saturday, just us girls. Do you think you can make it? Hope, Wanda, Hanna and a Townsend sister or two should be there."

"At your place?" Miranda asked.

"Yep. Early afternoon when the sun is warmest."

Miranda grinned, "Wouldn't miss it for the world."

THE WEDDING the night before had been a party to remember. Faith and Hunter had been stunning in their formal wedding gear, but what made it so special was the fact they had it at the spa they'd built together, and the place had been strung with thousands of fairy lights and candles. Shannon had never seen anything more beautiful. She'd spent the entire evening on the dancefloor with Brian and then the rest of the night with him in her bed.

Now she was sitting outside on one of her lounge chairs with five of her girlfriends, sipping mojitos and soaking up the sunshine.

"It's too bad Rex isn't staying in town," Wanda said. "That man is hot."

Hanna and Hope both nodded their agreement as they slathered on more sun screen.

"Where's he going?" Miranda asked, her face flushing slightly as she sucked down a big sip of her drink. Shannon grinned at her, knowing the woman was still embarrassed by the fact she'd felt him up that day at the shop.

"Christmas Grove," Yvette said. "He and Jacob have a friend there who owns a Christmas tree farm. Rex is going to give him a hand and help him heal a section of his farm that hasn't been performing very well."

"I've been to Christmas Grove once," Shannon said. "It's beautiful there. Such a sweet town, and the mountains are incredible."

"Me, too," Hanna said. "My parents used to take us during the holiday festivities. There's a reindeer games event that is hilarious. Air magic witches animate stuffed reindeer and there's a track and field event. I always wanted one as a pet until I realized they weren't actually real."

"It really is incredible," Yvette agreed. "Jacob and I are going out there right after Thanksgiving for a quick little getaway. You and Brian should come with us, Shannon. I'm sure Jacob and Rex would be thrilled."

Shannon laughed and shook her head. "I'm sure you and Jacob don't want us to crash your romantic getaway."

It was Yvette's turn to laugh. "Oh, no. It's not like that. Skye is coming with us. It's more of a family trip for a little fun. You guys should really come. It would be nice to spend a little more time with you when we all aren't so busy working."

"Well, when you put it that way—"

A collective gasp came from Shannon's friends and was followed by hoots and hollers and what she could only describe as catcalls. She jerked her head up and almost swallowed her tongue when she saw Brian strutting across the pool deck in only a thong.

"Work it!" Wanda called, pumping her fist in the air as Brian swayed his hips and strutted over to where the pool net was hanging on the side of an outbuilding.

"Flex! Show us the guns," Miranda added and started giggling when Brian took on a body builder's pose and started flexing his muscles for her.

"Wow, Shannon. You really bring the entertainment when you throw a party," Hope said with a laugh.

"Holy hell," Shannon whispered to herself as her chest exploded with pure love. Leave it to Brian to pay up on the bet he'd never lost.

"Whoa, Shannon," Yvette said. "He's got ripples on top of ripples. How do you stand yourself?"

Shannon grinned at her and shrugged noncommittally. It wasn't like Yvette wasn't married to a hottie of her own. Besides, she knew the other woman was mostly teasing. Or was she? Because damn, Brian looked incredible. Had he oiled up his muscles for an exaggerated effect? The way the sun was making him shine, it sure looked like it. She sat up and cried, "Show us your moves!"

Brian stopped flexing, looked right at her, winked, and then started twerking.

All of the women roared with laughter. By the time they finally calmed down, most of them were winded and had started to cry from laughing too hard.

Shannon got out of her chair and walked over to the man she would now forever refer to as the sexiest man alive and rewarded him with a searing kiss. Their audience came through with plenty of encouragement in the form of wolf whistles and chants of "get a room!"

When they finally pulled apart, Brian asked, "What was that for?"

"For being the best damned boyfriend that ever lived. Why in the heck would you put a G-string on and perform for my girlfriends?"

His eyes twinkled with mischief. "I wanted this day to be memorable."

"Oh, it's memorable all right. But why today?"

"Because Shannon Ansell, I have something to ask you." He got down on one knee, slid a platinum and diamond ring off his pinky finger, and held it up to her as he said, "I wasn't joking when I said I wanted to bring you to my sister's wedding as my fiancée. I have wanted you pretty much since the first time you flashed that gorgeous smile at me. I don't see that changing... well, ever. So I'm asking... will you marry me?"

Pleasure flooded her body from head to toe, and Shannon couldn't remember a moment that had ever been so perfect. "After seeing those twerking skills, I think I'd be crazy to say no."

He laughed. "Is that a yes then?"

"Yes."

Brian jumped to his feet, wrapped his arms around her, and swung her around with a joy that lit her up inside. One thing was for sure, whatever adventures were in store for her with Brian Knox, they were bound to never be boring.

"Oh my goddess!" Yvette called out, and at first Shannon thought she was just really happy for her and Brian. But then she said it again, and there was definitely a hint of panic in her voice when Shannon turned to see her speaking on her phone.

"What is it, Vette?" Wanda asked. "What's going on?"

"It's Noel. She's in labor. That little girl is coming today!"

Yvette hopped out of her chair and was quickly followed by the rest of the ladies, who were all close to Noel. They all wished her and Brian congratulations, apologized for cutting the pool date short, and then ran off to wait for what would probably be hours in the waiting room.

Brian followed Shannon into the house as the ladies left, and the moment the front door closed, he asked, "Is Silas here?"

"Nope. He's out with Levi for the day."

"Good." Brian scooped her up and took the stairs two at a time. "I have a fiancée to oil up."

CHAPTER 29

NOVEMBER

*R*ex Holiday walked behind his coupled-up friends through the enchanted town of Christmas Grove and knew he'd already fallen in love with the place. It wasn't all that different from Keating Hollow actually. Main Street was filled with quaint magic-oriented stores. There was Santa's Little Workshop, where toys seemed to be produced out of thin air, the Spellbound Bookstore, the Enchanted Bean Stalk that served everything from coffee to wheatgrass, and of course the Love Potions Chocolatier.

But what he loved most about the town were the people. They'd already run into the senior citizen polar bear club, which consisted of five older women who were committed to riding snowmobiles all winter and skinny dipping in Silver Moon Lake every chance they got from October through March. There were a group of teenagers taking it upon themselves to decorate the town with all things Christmas. And then there was the book club... four men, all of different ages, who delighted in picking outlandish titles for the group to read and then recommend to the rest of the town.

Everyone seemed happy, content. It was a state of being that had eluded Rex in the past. Sure, he'd had moments of those things, but they were fleeting. But this town... There was something about it that settled in his bones and made him think he could feel like that for forever.

It was too bad he had a job to get to in New York state come January. He would've liked to have tried living in Christmas Grove for a while.

Jacob paused and turned around, meeting Rex's eyes. "We're headed to the tree lighting ceremony. You up for that?"

"Sure. Let me stop in somewhere and get a drink. I'll meet the rest of you over in the square. Does anyone want anything while I'm poking around the stores?"

Jacob asked his wife, Yvette, and then Brian and Shannon, who were so loved up on each other Rex had trouble believing they'd even heard Jacob's question. It was sweet, if not slightly annoying. He'd had a bit of a crush on Shannon before he realized his buddy had his eye on her. Still, he conceded it was probably better Brian got to her first. Rex's track record with relationships was worse than mediocre. His longest relationship had lasted all of three months. Not very impressive for a thirty-five-year-old man, was it?

"We're good," Jacob said. "We'll be by the giant reindeer." He chuckled. "Skye wants to pet it."

"Of course she does. Look at it." He nodded toward the eight-foot-tall stuffed animal. It was a child's dream. "I'll be there in a few minutes."

Jacob nodded and ushered his small family, along with Shannon and Brian, toward the square.

Rex turned around and headed straight back toward the

Love Potions Chocolatier. There was a chocolate covered caramel square in the window that was calling his name. Because the tree-lighting ceremony was getting ready to begin, by the time he made it into Love Potions the place was empty except for one really pretty, curly-haired redhead who was leaning against the counter, waiting for help.

"Hello," Rex said as he joined her. "Have you seen anyone yet?" he asked curiously, just to make conversation. He didn't really care how long it took. He wasn't in any hurry to get anywhere. The tree was going to be just as sparkly an hour after they lit it, wasn't it?

"Sure," the woman said, scanning him from head to toe with her enchanting green eyes. "Mrs. Pottson is in the back getting my holiday cheesecake."

Feeling a little like she'd just looked at him with x-ray vision, Rex decided turnabout was fair play, so he took her in just as leisurely as she had him. Damn, she was gorgeous. Long, shapely legs, round hips, hourglass figure, and a face he could stare at for hours.

She laughed. "Like what you see?"

Her bluntness snapped him back to himself, and he grinned like a fool. There was nothing he liked better than a straight forward, direct woman. He supposed that was why he'd been interested in Shannon before she'd been removed from the dating pool. "As a matter of fact, yes. Your legs are incredible. Are you a dancer by chance?"

She tilted her head to one side to study him. "How did you know that? Do you dance, too?"

He shook his head. "Sadly, not even one step. My sister did it competitively for years though. You could say I've seen my fair share of dancers' legs."

"I bet."

Mrs. Pottson returned with the cheesecake box and handed it to the gorgeous creature in front of him. "Here you go, Holly. Sorry it took me so long. It was hiding behind the garden cake. You know how big those flowers grow."

Holly told the woman it was no problem and then when she turned to leave, she glanced at Rex. "It was nice chatting with you."

"Wait," Rex said, stepping into her path. He held out his hand. "I've only been in town a few weeks, and I don't think we've met yet. I'm Rex Holiday, and I'm here helping out my buddy at Frost's Christmas Tree Farm. Thought it might be nice to introduce myself."

Holly gave him a polite smile and shook his hand. When she let go, she said, "Holly Reineer. I'm not new in town. You can usually find me running the desk at the town library. It was nice to meet you Rex."

She spun on her heel, maybe a little too fast, and headed for the door.

"Hey, Holly?"

She paused and turned to look at him. "Yeah?"

"Would you maybe be interested in drinks or, better yet, dinner tonight?"

Those gorgeous green eyes flashed with something he was certain was interest. But it vanished just as fast as she said, "Sorry. I don't date temporary men."

The door swung open, and before he could think of a comeback, she was gone.

"Damn. It was worth a try," he said.

"It sure was, young man," Mrs. Pottson said.

Rex turned his attention to the round older woman with a kind face. "What did she mean by temporary? Is that some new insult I haven't been paying attention to?"

Mrs. Pottson laughed. "No, sweetie. It means she knows you aren't staying in this town for long."

He frowned. "How could she possibly know that?"

"Vision," she said simply. "Holly is always the first to know everything." She winked and then propped her arms up on the counter. "Now, what can I get for you today?"

"Whatever that chocolate covered caramel thing is that's advertised on the window and something to drink."

"Are you headed to the tree lighting ceremony?" she asked as she retrieved his chocolate.

"Yep. My friends are waiting there for me."

Mrs. Pottson nodded as if he'd just told her something important. Then she smiled and asked, "Do you like cider?"

"Sure."

"Good. One cup of Cupid's cider coming right up."

Five minutes later, Rex had his chocolate and his drink in hand and was weaving his way through the crowd trying to get to the giant stuffed reindeer that Skye loved so much. He spotted Brian and Shannon leaning against a railing and made a beeline for them. Within moments, he spotted Yvette and Jacob and Skye playing directly under the reindeer with another toddler who seemed fascinated with the giant beast. "I don't know how they do it," Rex said.

Brian followed his gaze until he spotted Jacob and Skye giggling like fools. "It's some sort of weird baby serum that parents just sort of end up with," he said, grinning at Rex. "They fall in love with those little monsters, and then they are lost to the dark side. Word of caution; If you don't want your days filled with stuffed animals and hair bows, keep it wrapped up."

Rex barked out a laugh and saluted his friend. "I'm on it, Captain."

"Good man," Brian said as he turned his attention to the woman who'd just stepped behind the microphone.

The pretty, light-haired woman was dressed almost exactly like Glenda the Good Witch from *The Wizard of Oz*. She wore a sparkling beige dress, a fancy crown, and carried a wand that was in the shape of a star. It was cheesy and adorable at the same time. She read a Christmas poem, sang a Christmas song that he'd never heard, and then ended with a sort of prayer. "May your nights be full of warmth and your days full of friendship. Let love in this holiday season, let it grow, and most of all believe. Happy holidays everyone!" She raised her glass and took a gulp.

Rex repeated her incantation and downed his cider. Immediately his limbs started to tingle, and he felt a little warmth in his chest. But both sensations vanished, and he was left with a sense of *longing*. He wasn't so sure that was the best emotion to come away with, but at least it was honest. He did want someone in his life, someone to call his own. He just wasn't sure he was ready for it.

"Holy hell, Rex. Did you drink a love potion?" Shannon asked.

"What? Why do you say that?" he asked, looking down at himself as if he expected to see a pink halo.

"You're glowing." She touched her finger to her chest. "Right here. X marks the spot."

This time when he looked down, he saw what she meant. A small circle of light was right where his heart was. He wondered what it meant.

Someone bumped him from behind, sending him forward.

"Oh, crap. I'm so sorry," the woman said, tugging on his hand to steady him.

All that tingling and warmth he'd felt after the tree

ceremony rushed from him and straight into Holly Reineer. She yanked her hand back, stared down at her palm, and cursed. Loudly.

"What is it?" Rex asked.

"You idiot. You just unwittingly hit me with a love potion."

"I did?" he asked, completely taken aback.

"You did, and now I'm going to have to spend the next four weeks trying to get rid of it. Like I said, I don't do temporary men. Thanks a lot, Rex." She stalked off, leaving him to admire her perfect backside.

A slow smile claimed Rex's lips as he considered her words and then thought, *We'll just see about that.*

DEANNA'S BOOK LIST

Pyper Rayne Novels:
Spirits, Stilettos, and a Silver Bustier
Spirits, Rock Stars, and a Midnight Chocolate Bar
Spirits, Beignets, and a Bayou Biker Gang
Spirits, Diamonds, and a Drive-thru Daiquiri Stand
Spirits, Spells, and Wedding Bells

Jade Calhoun Novels:
Haunted on Bourbon Street
Witches of Bourbon Street
Demons of Bourbon Street
Angels of Bourbon Street
Shadows of Bourbon Street
Incubus of Bourbon Street
Bewitched on Bourbon Street
Hexed on Bourbon Street
Dragons of Bourbon Street

Last Witch Standing Novels:

Soulless at Sunset
Bloodlust By Midnight
Bitten At Daybreak

Crescent City Fae Novels:
Influential Magic
Irresistible Magic
Intoxicating Magic

Witches of Keating Hollow Novels:
Soul of the Witch
Heart of the Witch
Spirit of the Witch
Dreams of the Witch
Courage of the Witch
Love of the Witch
Power of the Witch
Essence of the Witch

Witches of Christmas Grove:
A Witch For Mr. Holiday

Witch Island Brides:
The Vampire's Last Dance
The Wolf's New Year Bride
The Warlock's Enchanted Kiss
The Shifter's First Bite

Destiny Novels:
Defining Destiny
Accepting Fate

ABOUT THE AUTHOR

New York Times and USA Today bestselling author, Deanna Chase, is a native Californian, transplanted to the slower paced lifestyle of southeastern Louisiana. When she isn't writing, she is often goofing off with her husband in New Orleans or playing with her two shih tzu dogs. For more information and updates on newest releases visit her website at deannachase.com.

Made in United States
North Haven, CT
17 April 2023